ELEPHANTS IN THE EAST

'What happens if we can't save Tina?' Mandy murmured.

'Dr Kambo will put her to sleep,' Charles replied. 'It's kinder than letting her starve to death.'

'Maybe.' Mandy frowned, but she knew he was right. 'And Evie?'

'The baby elephant? If she lives, the troop will find her. She'll stick with other orphans from the bigger herd. The orphans are always lonely. They're the elephants who hang around on the outside of the herd.'

Mandy fell silent. So how would it be today when they found Tina? Would she live and lead them to her lost daughter? Or would the worst have to happen?

LUCY DANIELS

Elephants

— *in the* —

East

Illustrations by Jenny Gregory

Hodder
Children's
Books

a division of Hodder Headline plc

Special thanks to Jenny Oldfield
Thanks also to C. J. Hall, B.Vet.Med., M.R.C.V.S., for reviewing
the veterinary material contained in this book.

First published in Great Britain in 1997
by Hodder Children's Books

A Catalogue record for this book is available from the British Library

ISBN 0 340 68719 3

Typeset by Avon Dataset Ltd, Bidford-on-Avon, Warks

Printed and bound in Great Britain by
Clays Ltd, St Ives plc

Hodder Children's Books
a division of Hodder Headline plc
338 Euston Road
London NW1 3BH

One

'Now, that's *my* kind of animal!' Mandy Hope's father stood on the shore of Lake Kasanka and admired the hippopotamus.

Mandy smiled at her friend, James Hunter. The huge hippo lazed in the water, only his little round ears and wide nostrils showing above the surface.

'Not a care in the world. Eating and sleeping, sleeping and eating! That's my idea of heaven!'

The hippo opened his big pink mouth and yawned.

'Talking of sleeping...' Adam Hope

yawned too, then looked at his watch, 'it's time for my siesta!'

'Talking of *eating* . . .' James cut in, 'isn't it lunch-time?'

'Back to camp, then.' Mandy gave in and led the way from the lake, across the mud flat to the jeep. If it had been up to her, she would have stayed all day to watch the hippos. They were brilliant animals, with their piggy eyes and big fat bellies, their tiny trotters and stumpy legs.

A family of warthogs trotted across their path, tails up, snouts to the ground. They left a trail of neat footprints behind. Further off, a herd of zebra wandered down to the lake to drink.

'How long have we been here at Ruwenzori?' Mandy sighed, as she climbed into the jeep and sank back against the seat. 'Ten years?' She felt completely at home.

'Ten days.' James clambered in beside her, while Mr Hope started the engine. The jeep turned in a wide arc and made its way slowly between some tall thorntrees.

Mandy glanced at him. They'd come to Africa to stay with the Hopes' friend, Levina Lemiso, who was a scientist in the Ruwenzori Crater. Their real home was thousands of miles away in Yorkshire. 'Feeling homesick?' she asked.

'A bit.'

'Me too.' She thought of Gran and Grandad Hope tucked up in cosy Lilac Cottage with Smoky, their cat.

No doubt James was thinking of Welford, and Blackie, his disobedient Labrador. 'I wonder if Mum and Dad have got my postcard,' he murmured.

'Not yet,' Adam Hope said, as they drew clear of the thorntrees and within sight of Kampi ya Simba. 'It takes time for the post to get through. But we can drive into Arusha tomorrow, if you like, and telephone them from there.' Their jeep churned up clouds of red dust as they picked up speed. 'I have to phone Simon at Animal Ark, to check in and see how things are going there.'

Both Mandy's parents were vets in Welford, and however much the family were enjoying their African adventure, they couldn't forget the responsibilities of home.

'Thanks.' James cheered up. 'I wonder what's for lunch.'

'Eggs!' Mandy guessed. 'Scrambled eggs, boiled eggs, fried eggs, omelettes!' Eggs were always on the lunch-time menu.

'And count yourselves lucky.' Adam Hope reminded them not to take anything for granted out here in the bush.

James and Mandy leaped down and raced across the yard towards the research station. Thomas was already carrying plates on to the veranda, where Mandy's mum and Dr Lemiso sat in the shade.

'Egg sandwiches!' James announced, ready to tuck straight in.

'Hands!' Emily Hope reminded them.

They did a quick detour to the shower block to wash and disinfect them, then hared back to the long wooden hut. 'I'm starving!' Mandy sighed. She sank her teeth into the tasty sandwich.

'Is it good?' Thomas grinned at their appetites. He was Levina's cook, only a couple of years older than Mandy and James; a small, slight boy with a big, frequent smile and white, even teeth.

They nodded and went on munching.

'What did you see this morning?' Emily Hope asked. She and Levina had stayed behind to write up information about the migration of elephants from the Ruwenzori National Park. Levina was worried that the troops weren't travelling north into the mountains and on to the vast grasslands beyond, as they normally did at this time of year.

'Hippos.' Mandy was busy eating, so James answered. 'Nine altogether, including three babies.'

'Dad's favourite.' Mandy looked around for her father. She saw him stroking Danny, Thomas's pet duiker. The small, ugly deer lifted a thin back leg and scratched himself. 'You'd better be quick, Dad, before we eat all the sandwiches!'

'Coming.' He patted Danny's head between his little pointed horns and turned away. Humming to himself, he made for the shower block.

This time Danny lifted his front hoof and pawed the dusty ground. He was a solid little deer with red-brown hide and a wedge-shaped face beneath those pointed horns. He pricked up his ears at Mr Hope's humming.

'Da-ad!' Mandy called out as Danny lowered his head. The tune must have drowned out her voice. Adam Hope stood at the tap, his back to the duiker. He bent over to wash his hands. 'Watch out!'

Danny charged. *Whack*! His head made contact with Mr Hope's knees. Mandy's dad's legs buckled and he collapsed in a heap.

'Ouch!'

'Are you OK?' Mandy and James ran to pick Mr Hope out of the dirt, while Thomas dived after Danny.

'Fine!' The look of surprise lingered on his face. 'What was that?'

'Danny!' Mandy told him the harsh truth; 'I don't think he liked your singing!' As they brushed him down, James gave her a look that warned her not to laugh.

Thomas caught the duiker and told him off. 'Bad!' he said, raising a warning finger. 'You whack Mr Hope on the legs, he falls down; very bad!'

Mandy's lips trembled. Her dad was covered in red dust, his face was puzzled.

'Not like my singing?' Now he looked hurt. 'But I'm in the village choir!'

'That's back in Yorkshire.' Briskly, Levina came down into the yard to see that there was no real damage. Her green and orange traditional dress showed up the darkness of her skin. She spoke in a low, musical voice and arrived with a broad smile on her round face. 'Everything in Africa is different, remember!'

In Africa nothing was as you expected, Mandy knew. Here it was winter in July, and winter was hotter than Welford's summer. Since they'd arrived, she'd spent all day, every day, in T-shirt and shorts, baseball cap pulled firmly down to shade her face from the sun.

Every evening, after dark, she had to zip up

her fleece jacket to keep out the cold. Mists rolled down into the crater from the Ruwenzori Mountains in the north, and with them came a breeze. The Hopes and James would sit inside the research hut with Levina, Thomas and Joseph, the driver at the camp. They would play cards, tell stories, talk about the animals they had seen. Then they would walk out under a star-speckled sky, unzip their tents and curl up inside their warm sleeping bags. Within minutes they would all be sound asleep.

But that night, Mandy lay awake. Something had happened to make them put off the drive into Arusha next day. They'd been interrupted in the middle of a game of cards.

' . . . Snap!' Her dad had got in first and snatched the pile.

'We're only letting you win because we feel sorry for you,' Mandy had joked.

'How come?'

'Because Danny butted you.' She could hear Levina's radio transmitter beginning to crackle and whine. A message was coming through.

'Yeah, yeah.' Adam Hope had stacked his new cards into a neat pile.

'Hang on a second.' Mandy's mum thought

they should wait until Levina had taken the message.

They'd all listened in.

'*Jambo*, Matthew, how are you? . . . Yes, we're well, thank you.' Levina spoke loud and clear.

The voice of Matthew Mulakesi crackled across the airwaves from his home to the north of Lake Kasanka. Matthew was the chief warden in the Ruwenzori National Park. 'Levina, I wanted to let you know that a guest will be arriving in the crater early tomorrow morning.'

'By plane?' She knew that this would be the reason for Matthew's message. The only area flat enough for a small aircraft to put down in the crater was a patch of land close to her research station. 'Would you like Joseph to drive your guest across to the lodge?'

'Yes, please. His name's Fred Kambo. Have you met him?'

'He's the vet from Mombasa, isn't he?'

Mandy had pricked up her ears. Why would a vet be flown in from the city? Matthew knew that they already had two good vets here, in the shape of her own mum and dad.

'That's right. We want him to take a look at Tina.'

James had frowned at Mandy. 'Who's Tina?' he'd whispered.

She'd shrugged.

'Is she sick?' Levina had asked.

Matthew had hesitated and mumbled the word '*Shifta*!' Then he'd gone on speaking in Swahili.

'Ah!' Levina had looked serious. 'Yes, of course. Anything we can do to help.' She'd promised that Joseph would drive Dr Kambo to the lodge the moment he landed.

'Who's Tina?' James had asked, while Mandy had searched her memory for the meaning to the sinister-sounding word.

Shifta . . . shifta? Poachers! She remembered with a jolt.

'Tina's an adult female elephant in the troop that lives on the east side of the lake. She's been injured pretty badly, according to Matthew. They can't get near her to try and help, so he thought he'd better call in the expert.' Levina's normally cheerful voice had become slow and hesitant. 'Fred Kambo is the best elephant man around. If there's a bad problem up there with the troop, he's the one who can solve it.' She'd tried to put on a brave smile.

'*Shifta* means poacher, doesn't it?' Mandy had asked. She'd heard stories about the men who still crept into the national parks to hunt and kill valuable game. It was against the law to kill elephants for their ivory tusks, but the law didn't always stop the *shifta* from carrying out their cruel acts. 'Is it poachers who've hurt Tina?'

'Yes.' Levina wouldn't tell them any more until she knew all the details herself.

The message from the warden had ruined the easy-going mood of the evening, and they'd gone to bed early. And that was when Mandy's active imagination had got to work.

What if Tina died? The idea lodged itself in her brain. What if Dr Kambo didn't get there in time and she was too sick for him to save her? How badly was she hurt? Did Mr Mulakesi know exactly where to find her? She turned the questions over and over, staring up at the white canvas lining of her tent.

She tried to picture Tina. How old was she? Levina had called her an adult, but that could mean anything. Elephants lived for up to sixty years. Was she a mother? Perhaps she had young calves? In any case, the very idea of poachers harming one of these wonderful creatures stopped Mandy from falling asleep.

Elephants are the largest land mammal in the world. They can tear up whole trees with their trunks. They have long memories, they rumble, squeal and trumpet their way across the African grasslands. Mandy recited elephant facts to help her get to sleep. Mothers carry their young for almost two years before they give birth. They're unhappy when members of their family die.

Her mind kept coming round to sad ideas. Yet the elephants she'd seen whenever she'd been driving in the crater with Joseph had been playful, happy creatures. She'd watched them make friends, throw dust, splash mud and pick up the tiniest leaf with their snaking, agile trunks. She'd heard them bellow, roar and purr. She'd picked up meanings behind the sounds: a trumpeting call could mean 'Let's play' as well as, 'I'm angry', while a low rumble from deep in the chest meant anything from 'Let's go' to 'I'm pleased to see you'.

And Mandy had fallen in love with the creatures the moment she'd set eyes on them. It wasn't their saggy grey skins and great flappy ears. It wasn't the curling, swaying trunks or the funny little tufted tails. It was their eyes, she decided; those small, dark, shining intelligent eyes that seemed to wrinkle in a permanent, kindly smile. She thought of their long memories and their great wisdom, passed from one generation to the next, that set them apart from all the other wonderful animals she'd seen in Africa so far.

'It's almost as if they can talk!' she said to herself, moments before she drifted off to sleep at last.

Two

'We'll need all the help we can get,' Fred Kambo told them, soon after his plane had touched down at seven o'clock next morning.

Emily Hope had volunteered to go with him to the east side of the lake. 'I'm happy to be your assistant,' she told him. 'I don't know much about elephants, though. A Friesian cow in calf is the largest animal I've ever had to tackle!'

Dr Kambo smiled. 'Are you sure you want to get involved? I thought this was supposed to be a holiday for you.'

Mandy and James hovered in the yard,

listening. The grown-ups had gathered on the veranda.

'A working holiday,' Adam Hope explained. He too had asked if he could help, all jokes about wallowing and lazing in the sun like the hippos forgotten.

The vet from Mombasa admitted that he was glad. He wasn't what Mandy had been expecting. Dr Kambo sounded like a man in a suit, with a collar and tie. In fact, their visitor was wearing jeans and a blue sweatshirt that had a surfing logo splashed across the back. He was about the same age as her parents, but much smaller and stockier than her dad. He spoke perfect English.

'What about us?' James whispered to her as they went on discussing which track they should take to find the injured elephant. 'Do you think they'll let us go, too?'

'Oh, if only!' She longed to ask, but knew the treatment of this elephant was far too urgent to delay. 'We'd better let them get on without pestering them.'

So they watched in silence as Joseph brought the jeep up to the porch and they began to load it up.

'How long will we be?' Emily Hope asked, bringing food for the journey. 'Will we need our sleeping bags?'

'No, we should manage the job in one day,' the newcomer told her. 'If not, we'll head up to the warden's lodge and stay there. But I have to be back in Mombasa by tomorrow night, so I can't spend more than one night there.'

Mandy swivelled her eyes sideways to look at James. A night in the foothills of the Ruwenzori Mountains! The Mountains of the Moon. 'Wow!' she breathed. 'That sounds even better than camping by the lake!' They'd already done that, when they'd taken Safi, the lion-cub, to rejoin his family.

'I spoke to Matthew on the radio last night, and he says the best plan is for us to take the track up the west side of the lake, meet him at the northernmost point, then head east to-gether, out to where he last saw the injured elephant. He reckons we should get there before midday.' After explaining, Fred left them for a few moments and went to talk to Levina inside her office.

Meanwhile, Thomas flew round the camp, handing out mugs of scalding hot tea, while

Joseph opened up the bonnet of the jeep to check the engine.

Adam Hope took his tea and came quickly across, keeping a wary eye open for Danny the duiker. 'Sorry about the drive into town,' he told James. 'We'll do it as soon as I get back.'

'That's OK, thanks.'

'And, Mandy, try not to worry. We'll take the portable radio with us and get a message back as soon as we've been able to find this elephant and treat her. We'll just have to hope that everything's going to turn out all right.' He gave her one of his kind, lop-sided grins.

She nodded, wishing with every fibre of her being that she and James were going with them. At home in Welford, she was sure they would have been allowed to go along. But here in Africa, with an expert flown in specially to treat Tina, she knew it would be wrong to push themselves forward.

Fred Kambo came down the two steps in one stride, waving goodbye to Levina, and ready to go. He gestured for Adam and Emily Hope to climb into the back of the jeep, then hitched himself up beside them. Glancing round, he noticed James and Mandy standing in the grey morning light.

'What are you two waiting for?' he demanded.

They trotted across the yard. 'What do you mean?' Mandy caught a glimmer of humour in the vet's eyes.

'Well, hop in if you want to come with us,' he said, as if he'd been expecting it all along. 'There's plenty of room!'

The sentence was hardly out of his mouth before Mandy had flung open the passenger door and jumped up beside Joseph. 'Thanks!' A smile spread across her tanned face.

James joined her and slammed the door shut. He pulled his cap out of his jacket pocket and rammed it down over his forehead, hanging on to the roll-bar as the jeep lurched forward. 'Wow!' he said. In Africa, every day *was* different.

The sun rose higher and turned the grey sky pink, then golden, then pure blue. Joseph took them down as close to the lakeside as he could to find the flattest land for driving, then hurtled across the pebbled beaches and mudflats, raising flocks of startled flamingoes as they sped by. Small gazelles leaped up in the air as if their legs were on springs. They scattered in all directions. Monkeys swung up into the thorntrees and chattered angrily.

'Sorry!' Mandy hung out of the window to take it all in; the black faces of the monkeys peering down at them, the vultures rising from the flat treetops, two rhinos lumbering off ahead of the jeep like dinosaurs that history had left behind. Their thick skin hung in leathery folds, their tiny eyes peered blindly ahead as they lowered their curved horns and charged away. 'We didn't mean to scare you!'

The jeep cut through the dry landscape like a great metal monster. The spear-shaped leaves of seisal bushes and giant cactus trees loomed on either side. She drew her head back inside the car and stared out across the lake.

'She's over there somewhere,' Fred Kambo said, guessing her thoughts. 'East of the lake is where Tina's troop normally lives in the dry season. Ordinarily, they would begin to head north about now, on to the plains beyond the mountains. Elephants like moist, open grass-land. They can smell rain at a great distance. In the old days of open migration, they were known to walk five hundred kilometres in herds of up to one thousand animals, following the rain.'

'What was open migration?' James asked. He still held on to the bar as the jeep dipped and rocked across the rough country.

'Before we had the national parks in East Africa, all the big game could roam freely. Now they live mostly in protected areas, managed by wardens.'

'Why?' Mandy was curious. Africa was a vast, empty continent. Surely there was still enough space for the animals to roam wherever they wanted.

'Man,' Fred said abruptly.

'That old problem.' Mandy's mum hung on tight and watched the reaction of a herd of zebras to their speeding vehicle.

'I'm afraid so. Believe it or not, until the 1970s there were too many elephants in this part of Africa. Then the price of ivory shot up and the poachers moved in.'

Mandy turned to listen, swaying and rocking with the movements of the car.

'The ivory trade is one of the tragedies of this continent. Poaching has put paid to hundreds of thousands of these magnificent creatures, and when you put this together with their loss of habitat—'

'Meaning?' Adam Hope interrupted quickly.

'The cutting down of trees to make way for coffee plantations, cattle farms and so on – well, then by the end of one more decade, the poor old elephant was actually an endangered species. Numbers are still dropping each year, in spite of everything the governments are trying to do to conserve them. Now they mostly exist in the national parks. Gone are the days when elephants could wander free . . .'

Mandy sighed. More sad stories. She'd heard so often that the elephants were having a hard time.

'Do the wardens know every single elephant in their park?' James wanted to know. 'I mean, does each one have a name, for instance?'

Fred nodded. 'They recognise them by the small differences. One elephant's ears can be bigger than another's, one can have a smaller trunk, or a more humped back. It's easy for an expert to tell them apart.'

James listened in silence.

'They're like people, then?' Mandy asked.

Fred smiled. 'What elephant do you know who would wear a necklace made out of your teeth round his neck?'

'Ouch!' she grimaced.

'Exactly. But people make ornaments out of ivory, don't they? You see, elephants are kinder than some people.' He leaned forward and tapped Joseph's shoulder. 'Is that the warden's jeep over there?'

They all followed his pointing finger and spotted a trail of dust in the distance. Joseph nodded and altered course. Soon the two jeeps met up and everyone jumped out.

'*Jambo! Habari?*' There was an outburst of greetings in Swahili. 'Hello, how are you?' They shook hands with Matthew Mulakesi, and two more wardens called Huanga and Abekuna; both tall, wiry men from the Masai tribe.

'You won't believe how glad we are to see you!' the head warden told Fred Kambo. 'Huanga and Abekuna spent the night down on the eastern shore, keeping an eye on Tina.'

'How is she?' Fred asked Mandy and James to help lift some equipment from the jeep.

'Still losing blood from the wound. She must be pretty weak by now.'

'I take it we can't get any closer by car?'

'No. We have to walk from here. There are no tracks along this shore, and it's pretty rocky. It's a trek of about four kilometres. We should do it in just over an hour.'

'What do you want me to carry?' Mandy asked, eager to set off as soon as possible. She took a bag full of medicines and dressings and slung it across her shoulder. She saw that the two Masai men carried long, stout sticks to beat back the undergrowth. Her mum and dad took their own vets' bags, though they would have to wait for Fred Kambo to give the orders. Meanwhile, James took up the rucksack of food.

'How did it happen exactly?' Fred wanted to know. They'd set off along the water's edge, and walked in silence until they'd rounded the northern tip of the lake and headed south down the eastern side.

'No one actually saw it.' Matthew swung his own strong stick against the undergrowth of seisal leaves and bright orange convolvulus flowers. 'But we heard the elephant's screams all the way up at the lodge. We knew straight away what it was.'

Mandy frowned and ducked her head to avoid

an overhead creeper. James caught his foot in a crevice in the rock, stumbled, then carried on.

'Did you know there were poachers in the area?' Emily Hope asked. She walked ahead of Mandy, looking all around for any sign of the elephant they were seeking.

'We didn't see any. But we did wonder why the troop hadn't migrated north. It was time for them to be leaving the crater, but they seemed not to want to risk the mountain passes. It was as if they knew there was danger up there. Anyway, the *shifta* must have got tired of waiting and come right down into the park to get what they wanted.'

'Ivory?' James asked quietly.

Matthew nodded. 'The way these men work is to separate the animal they want from the rest of the group, then spear her. They target the soft area under her belly, just in front of her back leg. But in this case their aim was bad. They got her in the left leg, just above the knee. She was wounded but not killed. The screaming we heard was part fear, part anger. And I wouldn't be surprised if the other elephants didn't come charging back to help Tina. In any case, the poachers didn't hang around long enough to finish her off, and what we're left with is a badly injured elephant, a scared troop, and a bunch of poachers who've been cheated of their kill ever since we showed up to keep an eye on things.'

The warden finished, but for a while no one spoke. Mandy felt the anger boil up inside her.

'Oh, and one other thing—' Matthew held up his hand in a silent order to stop. He finished off the bad news in a low whisper. 'We know that Tina was looking after a calf of eighteen months; a young female called Evie. But since the incident happened, there's been no sign of the youngster. Huanga has had a good sighting of the rest of the troop and she's definitely not with them.'

Mandy bit her lip. 'Could the poachers have got her?'

The warden shrugged. 'We don't know. There wouldn't be any ivory for them; she's too young. But, in any case, a baby elephant's chances of surviving alone are less than fifty-fifty. Even if the *shifta* didn't injure or kill her, she's definitely managed to get herself lost.'

'Why have we stopped?' James whispered. He pushed his cap back and wiped his forehead.

Up ahead, Huanga was pointing towards the lake. Glad of the rest, unsuspecting, they turned to look.

'Elephants!' Mandy gasped, then breathed out with a low cry. In spite of the gruesome story that Matthew had just told them, she couldn't help being excited by the sight of the giant creatures less than two hundred metres away, standing in the shallows at the edge of the shimmering blue and silver expanse.

There were a dozen or more drinking and bathing in the morning sun. Young males strode in and sucked water up through their trunks.

One squirted a jet into his mouth, another waved his trunk like a hose and sprayed it over his dry back. Bigger females took it more slowly, coaxing smaller calves in, or drawing them close with their waving trunks. So far the troop didn't seem to have spotted the warden and his group.

'Is it Tina's group?' James whispered.

Matthew nodded. 'They're on edge,' he warned. 'And who can blame them?'

'Are you sure Tina's baby isn't there?' Mandy was hoping that the lost youngster had been found.

The warden counted and studied each of the young calves. 'No.' He shook his head sadly.

Just then, Abekuna came up from the back of their procession. 'Let's go!' he whispered.

'Why, what's the problem? Have they spotted us?' Fred Kambo narrowed his eyes to study the elephants' behaviour. One of the strong young males was lifting his trunk and scenting the air. The other adults flapped their ears and turned their massive heads towards the bushes where Mandy's group crouched and watched. Then an ear-splitting roar tore through the air.

'What do we do now?' Adam Hope asked the wardens. 'I don't know too much about elephants, but they look to me as if they're about to charge! And they can scoop you up on those tusks and toss you thirty metres or more!'

'Who says they'll charge?' Mandy tried to sound braver than she felt. The roar had been so angry that she couldn't stop herself from trembling.

'We can't be sure, but I think we should get out of here,' Matthew advised. 'After what happened yesterday, these elephants are not about to trust anyone!'

So they left the cover of the thorn bushes and began to follow Huanga up a slope, running as fast as they could. More elephants began to trumpet and roar, there was a loud splashing and tramping of huge feet. Mandy glanced back at the cloud of white spray churned up by the angry elephants.

'Quickly!' Emily Hope urged her and James to scramble up to the safety of more thick thorn bushes on a ledge of red rock.

'Definitely worse than being charged by a duiker!' Mr Hope gasped. They'd managed to reach the ledge, and stood breathing hard, staring down at the still restless animals. But the noise was dying down and they were going back to the business of drinking and bathing.

'Danger's passed!' Mandy's mum said with a relieved sigh.

Matthew shook his head. 'I don't like it.'

'Wouldn't they normally behave like that?' Emily asked. 'After all, we are strangers to them.' She turned to the expert for advice.

The warden shook his head. 'These elephants know us. They've even been known to come to the lodge for help if one of them is in trouble. Believe me, they can tell their friends from their enemies. Until now.' He spoke sadly, then pulled himself together. 'Well, let's show them we still mean well. Maybe if we can treat Tina, they'll forget about the *shifta* and learn to trust us again.'

And so they set off, hotter than ever after their sprint up the hill, more subdued, and frightened of what they might find when finally they reached the place where the injured elephant lay.

Three

'There she is; she's still on her feet!' Fred Kambo saw Tina before any of the others.

Mandy peered up the hillside. There was a trail of damage; flattened grass, broken branches on the thorn bushes the injured creature had crashed through. And then she saw the elephant herself. She was about a hundred metres off, and limping away from them, struggling up the hill in a desperate effort to get away.

'The left leg's swollen,' Emily Hope pointed out. Their group had immediately stopped trying to follow Tina. Now they waited for her to recognise Matthew and the other wardens as her friends. 'How are we going to get near her?'

'With this.' Fred Kambo asked Adam Hope to help him prepare and load a powerful-looking tranquilliser gun.

'Poor thing!' Mandy could hardly bear to look. There was a huge gash in the elephant's leg, just above the knee. She'd staggered to a halt, head and trunk raised, ready to limp off again if any of them took a step in her direction.

'I need to be closer,' Fred said, quietly.

'You try and creep up on her from behind,' Matthew suggested. 'The rest of us will stay here and distract her.'

The vet nodded, shouldered his gun and slid off into the cover of some thick cactus bushes. Meanwhile, Tina kept a wary eye on Mandy and the others.

'I hope he makes it quick,' she whispered under her breath. Waiting for Fred Kambo to fell the elephant with the tranquilliser dart felt like torture. Even though it was a case of being cruel to be kind, Mandy couldn't help feeling that Tina wouldn't see it that way. All she would know would be a shot, dizziness, and then she would collapse on the ground in confusion. 'This is horrible,' she said to James.

'Don't worry, once the dart is fired, it'll only take a little while to work.' Mrs Hope put an arm round Mandy's shoulder.

They waited. Minutes ticked by with only the buzz of insects in the air, and the swish of Tina's trunk as she swayed unsteadily and kept her distance.

Then there was the crack of a gun. A dart landed in the elephant's haunch. Its red tag fluttered to show the vet that his aim had been good. Tina whipped her trunk into the air in fresh panic, and tried to tug herself up the hill. After only a few metres, her legs failed her. She sank slowly to the ground.

Then they all began to run towards her, covering the rocky ground as the elephant collapsed on to her left side. Mandy and James were faster and more nimble than the adults. They reached Tina at the same time as Dr Kambo, who stepped out of hiding and stood over her, shaking his head.

Mandy stopped dead. The sheer size of the elephant was amazing. Tina lay on her side. Her head was as big as an armchair, her trunk as thick as a man's waist. A musty smell of chewed grass hit their nostrils; sickly sweet and mixed with the earthy smell of dust.

The rest of the group soon joined them, and Matthew Mulakesi reached out his hand and laid it on the creature's wrinkled hide. 'Bad luck,' he said to the vet.

'What's gone wrong?' James asked him.

'Well, the tranquilliser worked well enough. It's M99; the strongest we have. Fatal to humans, of course, but strong enough to knock out the elephant and keep her down for a couple of hours. Unfortunately, she went down on the wrong side.'

Mandy and James realised what he meant. Tina had collapsed on to her left side, and now the injured leg lay hidden beneath her.

'Do we have any ropes to try and pull her over?' Fred asked Matthew.

The warden shook his head. 'Anyway, we could never do it with just eight of us. It takes at least ten men to lift an elephant.'

Huanga and Abekuna nodded in agreement. They too were shaking their heads.

'Can't we do anything?' Mandy pleaded. She stood beside Tina's head, so close that she could have touched her smooth, broad forehead.

Emily Hope dropped to her knees for a better look. She managed to glimpse the wound. 'It's infected,' she reported to the others. 'And it looks deep. But she isn't losing any more blood from it.' Next to the elephant's belly and hind leg, she was dwarfed. She tried to ease one arm under the leg, but failed to even shift it.

Fred nodded. 'Let's give her a shot of antibiotic while she's out. You'll be OK doing this,' he told Mandy's dad. 'It's the same as with any other large animal.'

Adam Hope stepped forward to inject the drug.

'How long will she stay unconscious?' James asked. He stood further back than Mandy, taking everything in.

'Two hours. But there's no point leaving her as long as that.' Dr Kambo was resigned to injecting the antidote to the M99 and getting Tina back on to her feet without dressing the wound. 'I'll give her this and make sure she comes round all right, then we'll have to leave her in peace, give her twenty-four hours to recover, and come back tomorrow to try again.' He went ahead with another needle, then told them all to stand well back.

Mandy and James did as they were told. But first, Mandy couldn't resist reaching out to stroke the elephant. She put the palm of her hand against Tina's cheek. The skin was dry and warm. 'We *will* come back to help you,' she promised quietly. Then she stepped back with the rest.

They watched as the antidote took effect. For a while Tina lay still. Then her tail began to twitch and flick. She shook her head. Slowly, with a huge effort, she pulled herself back on to her feet.

Mandy breathed a sigh of relief to see her upright once more.

'Let's go,' Matthew said, anxious to let the elephant recover quietly.

So they shouldered their bags and began to make their way down to the shore. When Mandy turned for a last look, Tina was already limping towards some trees, stretching her trunk and curling it round a low branch. At least she could still feed. 'Are you sure she'll be safe?' she asked the chief warden.

'Maybe.' He walked on, head down.

'Why? Nothing will attack an elephant, will it?' She couldn't imagine that even a lion or a leopard would hunt anything so huge.

'No, but I'm worried about the state of the wound,' he confessed. 'One shot of antibiotic may not be enough.' He turned to wait for Emily Hope, a deep frown on his face.

'Yes,' she agreed. 'The wound was very dirty. The infection's likely to be serious.'

Matthew sighed. 'Well, we'll have to see.'

As they went on in the full heat of the sun, along the edge of the lake, heading back north towards the warden's lodge, Mandy tried to find out what would happen next. 'What if the infection spreads?' she asked quietly.

Her mother understood what she wanted to know. 'Well, if we come back tomorrow and it turns out to be too bad to treat—' She turned to Dr Kambo for his opinion.

'If it's spread to the bone and into the whole of her system, the only kind thing to do will be to put her down,' he said, quietly.

Mandy nodded, too upset to say any more. They walked on and she didn't even notice the flamingoes lifting their wings in a brilliant display of red underfeathers, or the delicate striped duikers drinking at the water's edge. They walked straight past a family of hippos wallowing in the mud.

Mandy's eyes were full of tears, and her thoughts were with poor Tina limping up the hillside, struggling to survive.

Four

Ruwenzori Lodge was a long, low building made of concrete blocks. A porch ran along the front, and the roof was made of rusty corrugated iron. The lodge perched on a hill overlooking the northern tip of the lake, and was surrounded by cacti and banana trees whose broad, shiny green leaves gave plenty of shade from the fierce sun.

When Mandy and the rest of her party arrived there early in the afternoon, there seemed to be no one around. It was so still, hot and quiet that the brown earth shimmered. Even the Mulakesis' thin dog lay full length on the porch, not bothering to come and greet them. Instead, his tail wagged lazily, sweeping the boards and raising a small cloud of dust.

'*Karibu*!' Matthew said. 'Welcome. Come inside and meet Joan.'

Tired and thirsty, and above all disappointed with the morning's events, they trooped into the lodge. Matthew's wife greeted them and soon had them drinking sweet herb tea, sitting on the floor of a cool room with their backs resting against the smooth walls. Mandy sighed and relaxed. There was nothing more they could do for Tina until tomorrow. Meanwhile, she began to take in her surroundings.

Matthew and Joan's living-room was almost empty of furniture. There were no pictures on the walls, and only one small window covered by a blind made from woven palm leaves. They drank the tea out of shallow dishes, and watched as Joan and one of her daughters brought bowls of rice and vegetables and placed them in the middle of the floor.

'Please eat,' Joan said simply. She went away and brought back plates and another bowl full of fish grilled over a charcoal fire. 'There's plenty for everyone.'

By now, Mandy found she was hung... skipped breakfast, she remembered, a... walked a long way since they'd abando... jeeps and continued on foot. She spoone... the food on to her plate and tucked in. Soon, another of Matthew's children came shyly into the room; a girl of about five in a bright pink dress. Her eyes were big and round, fringed with long, curled lashes.

Mandy smiled at her. 'What's your name?'

The little girl didn't answer.

'She's called Ruth,' Matthew said. 'When she begins school she'll learn English, like my other daughter, Josephine, and my son, Charles.'

Josephine stooped to collect the empty plates. She looked pleased and embarrassed by the mention of her name. Like her younger sister, Ruth, her eyes were wide and dark, her skin smooth, her hair short and tightly curled. She smiled at Mandy as she stacked the plates.

'I can show you your room,' she offered, waiting at the door for Mandy to follow her. She looked about twelve years old and wore a white T-shirt over her orange, wraparound, traditional skirt.

Mandy thanked Matthew and Joan for her

meal and followed the girl outside. They went across the dirt yard and into a separate concrete building, split into small rooms. Josephine showed Mandy into one of them. Inside there were two wooden beds with shallow mattresses covered with white sheets. Over each bed, suspended from hooks in the low ceiling, was a spotless mosquito net.

'This is your bed for tonight, and this is mine,' the girl explained.

'Thanks.' She found that she'd caught Josephine's shyness and fumbled for something to say. 'Where do you go to school?' she asked.

'At Gamunde village, in the mountains. With my brother also.'

Mandy perched on the edge of one of the beds. 'How old is he?'

'Thirteen years. Soon he will leave school and start work with my father.' Josephine began to back out of the room.

'What about you? What will you do?'

'Help my mother. One day I hope to work in a hotel in Arusha.' The idea lit up her face with a bright smile. She stopped in the doorway and studied Mandy. 'How is England?' she murmured.

'What's it like?' Mandy thought hard about what Josephine would most like to hear. 'It's small compared with Africa – and cold.'

'Many cities? Many cars?'

She nodded. 'But I live in a small village.'

'Do you have a lake where you live?'

'No, but we have a river and hills. Yorkshire is very beautiful, too,' she told her. 'We have snow in winter.'

Josephine's eyes sparkled. 'I've seen snow on our mountains, very far off!' She turned her head to listen to something out in the yard. 'My brother, Charles, is back from school.' She beckoned Mandy to join her.

A boy in a white shirt and blue trousers was riding a bike towards the lodge. He came up the rough track, between seisal bushes, sitting upright on his shiny bicycle and pedalling hard.

'*Jambo!*' Josephine stepped into the yard, while little Ruth came running from the house.

More cries of '*Jambo!*' rang out, as Charles stopped his bike and scooped the little girl up on to the handlebars. Then he set off and wobbled towards the house.

Ruth squealed and laughed.

Suddenly, the quiet yard had come alive.

Adam and Emily Hope had finished their meal and came out with James on to the porch. From another concrete building, half-hidden by tall bushes, came Huanga with his wife and two children. They brought slices of mango and a pot of golden honey. The lazy dog on the veranda stretched and loped across to join them. Soon, everyone was smiling, eating and talking at once.

'*This* is what I like about Africa!' Mandy's dad sighed. He had squatted on the porch step, a slice of mango in his hand. 'It's not only animals, is it?' He turned to Mandy to check how she was feeling.

'No,' she admitted, 'this is great, too.'

Now though, there was something new going on in the middle of the yard. Abekuna had come out of one of the houses with a tall drum, settled himself cross-legged on the ground and begun to tap a gentle rhythm. The children crowded round him in their bright dresses and shorts.

The beat of the drum grew louder, joined by another one carried out from Huanga's house. Then Charles brought one too and soon the beat was complicated with cross-rhythms as three pairs of hands beat loudly, heads dipped and swayed and the girls and women began to sing.

Mandy closed her eyes to listen. The pounding rhythm seemed to get right inside her head. 'Yep,' she said, beginning to tap her feet to the main beat. 'This is Africa, all right!'

The next day was a Saturday. As Mandy and James got ready to set off on the second attempt to find Tina and treat her injured leg, they heard Charles Mulakesi asking his father if he could go too. He went back into the house, and five minutes later came out again with a smiling Josephine.

'We can both go,' she told Mandy.

'Like I said before, the more the merrier,' Fred Kambo said, as he passed by with a businesslike look. 'Are we all ready?' he asked the assembled group.

Joan picked Ruth up and stood at the door to wave them off. 'Good luck!' she cried. Huanga and Abekuna's wives and small children echoed the words.

The procession set off again, down to Lake Kasanka and along its eastern shore. They walked mostly in silence, thinking now of the task that lay ahead. James strode on beside Abekuna, so Mandy fell in beside Josephine and Charles as they walked in the shadow of giant ant-hills that rose like fairytale castles with towers and pointed peaks. The old question from the day before was nagging at her. 'What happens if we can't save Tina?' she murmured.

'Dr Kambo will put her to sleep,' Charles replied. He was matter-of-fact. 'It's kinder than letting her starve to death.'

'Maybe.' Mandy frowned, but she knew he was right.

'The other elephants will come and cover her body with branches,' he went on. 'They don't let the vultures come and peck at her. It's one of the wonders about them.'

Mandy didn't like to think about it. 'And Evie?'

'The calf? If she lives, the troop will find her. She'll stick with other orphans from the bigger herd.'

'Would she miss her mother?' Mandy wondered just how close to humans these intelligent animals might be.

This time Josephine was the one to answer. 'Yes. My father says that orphans are always lonely. They're the elephants who hang around on the outside of the herd. And when they grow up, they don't make good parents.'

'They don't know how,' Charles explained. 'Who can teach them if their mother's dead?'

Mandy fell silent. So how would it be today when they found Tina? Would she live and lead them to her lost daughter? Or would the worst have to happen?

They came across her not far from where they'd left her the day before. She stood hunched miserably in the long grass, a few hundred metres up the slope from the shore. She was alone. When she saw them, she raised her trunk and whipped it through the air.

They stopped at once and gathered round to watch Fred prepare the dart-gun once again.

'*Dawa*,' Charles said quietly, glancing up at the frightened elephant. 'This is good medicine.' They all felt the tension rise as Tina struggled off up the slope.

Today the vet knew there was no time to lose. 'No point creeping up,' he said. 'She's too weak to charge or even to run away. I can walk up to her, poor old girl.'

He went ahead up the hill.

Tina bellowed at him to keep his distance. She tried to tug herself away on her wounded leg.

Mandy put a hand to her mouth; it seemed so cruel to see the man advancing with his gun. He raised it and fired. The dart pierced the elephant's skin. She stood for a minute, then slowly sank back on to her haunches, going down in a strange sitting position, with her front legs raised.

'Is that it?' James asked, his voice strained. They all stared and waited for Tina to topple sideways.

'It looks like it.' Adam Hope went quickly to join Fred Kambo. 'Yes, she's out cold!' he called.

'Bring some ropes!' Dr Kambo issued the orders to Abekuna, Matthew and Huanga. He asked them to tie one to each of the elephant's tusks and told everyone to take a position, ready to pull or push Tina on to her right side.

Mandy swallowed hard. She heard Matthew say that the elephant weighed over two thousand kilogrammes. Now they must push her sideways so that the vets could treat her injury. As Dr Kambo gave the order to begin, Mandy rested her weight against Tina's left side and started to shove.

They strained to shift the weight; ten people to one elephant. She sat like a huge stone statue, pulled this way and that, until at last she began to topple. She crashed on to her side as they leaped clear, flattening bushes and thudding against the earth.

Then there was silence. Fred Kambo moved in and eased the huge flap of her left ear forward to cover her eye.

'Why did he do that?' James whispered to Charles.

'To keep the sun out of her eye.' The warden's son crept nearer, ready to help if needed.

Mandy and James followed him. They smelled the same smell as before, of sweet chewed grass and dust. But when Mandy saw the wound close to, she almost shied away again. Tina's whole knee joint was swollen, and the gash above it was long and open. Adam Hope handed Fred some plastic gloves and put a pair on himself.

'How bad is it?' Matthew asked, voicing the question on everyone's lips. 'Can we still save her?'

'We can have a go,' Fred decided. 'I don't

think the bone is infected at any rate.'

Mandy glanced at Josephine. They breathed sighs of relief.

'We have to clean the wound,' Emily Hope explained, as she too put on some gloves. 'Hand me those tweezers from my bag, please, Mandy.'

Mandy managed to do as she was told, watching as her mother began to pull dirt and grass from the wound. Then Dr Kambo moved in with surgical scissors and started to snip away at the infected flesh. Mr Hope finished off with disinfectant solution and a squirt of antibiotic.

'That's better!' Fred Kambo stood back to inspect their work. 'All we need now is a dusting of powder to keep away the insects.' He applied it from a tin with holes pierced in the top. 'Now for the antidote. Stand back, everyone!'

'More strong *dawa*!' James used the Swahili word as he spoke to Charles.

Fred injected the antidote to the anaesthetic and then they waited for Tina to come round.

They waited and waited. Mandy glanced at her dad, who shook his head, mystified.

'Another shot?' Emily Hope suggested.

Dr Kambo shook his head. 'Do we have any water?'

Mandy went forward with her own water bottle.

'Splash it on her face,' the vet told her.

Gingerly she unscrewed the top and poured water into her palm. She sprinkled it gently on to Tina's huge head.

'More.'

She did it again.

This time Tina opened her eyes and shook her head.

'Stand back!' Adam Hope warned.

They all retreated to watch the elephant recover.

First she raised her head. Keeping the on-lookers within her sights, she pushed herself up on to her forelegs, then heaved her massive weight clear of the ground. She stood up with a groan and a rumble from deep in her chest.

'Brilliant!' James breathed, pushing his cap back from his forehead.

'She's still shaky!' Mandy whispered.

Tina tested her weight on her injured left leg, curling her trunk back to sniff at the antiseptic medicines they'd used to help it to heal. She seemed surprised to find that the leg could already stand some of her weight.

'That's right; you'll soon be able to use it again.' Fred Kambo was satisfied with their morning's work. He began to pack his equipment back into his bag. 'Well done, everyone. Thank you very much.'

'Will she really be OK?' Mandy could still hardly believe that their treatment would work.

'Yes. Matthew and the others will have to keep an eye on her for a while, but there's no reason why she shouldn't be back to normal within a few days.'

It was like a weight easing from her, the knowledge that the magnificent elephant would soon be better. Mandy lifted her gaze to scan the hillside. There was plenty of food for Tina to eat; small trees and bark, a slope covered with grass and shrubs. She felt proud that she had played a part, however small.

But – and there was a big 'But' hanging in the air . . . Mandy searched the long slope. She listened for a faint call, looked and looked again for a clue that there was another elephant up there; a baby crying for her mother. Nothing. The grass rustled in the faint breeze. No sign of little Evie.

'Where *is* she?' James had come up beside her

and shielded his eyes against the sun. They searched the empty landscape.

Mandy shook her head. As Tina eased her way slowly down to the water, turning her back on the hill, they both scanned the slope in vain for her lost baby.

Five

Back at the wardens' lodge, Fred Kambo made radio contact with Levina at Kampi ya Simba. 'Tina will be fine,' he told her. 'I expect she'll rest up for a while, then rejoin the troop.'

'What about the calf?' The question came muffled and crackly over the airwaves.

Mandy, James and Charles sat together on the porch step, listening in to the conversation.

'No luck there, I'm afraid,' Dr Kambo replied. 'But Matthew has promised to keep a lookout over the next few days.'

'So your job's done up there?' Levina began to make arrangements to send the jeep to collect the vet, along with the Hopes and James. Joseph would drive out from camp and meet them at the same point as before.

'I need to fly out to Mombasa this evening,' Fred reminded her. 'My pilot's due to touch down in the crater at four this afternoon.'

Mandy glanced at her watch. It was one o'clock, and they would have to hurry for Dr Kambo to be on time to catch his small, two-seater plane. She sighed and stroked the Mulakesis' thin brown dog, Jonjo. Across the yard, two girls washed clothes at the tap, while Huanga sat smoking a cigarette in the shade of a huge baobab tree.

'We'd better get a move on,' James said.

'Yes, worse luck.' To Mandy it felt bad to be leaving the lodge before Evie had been found.

'I know.' James nodded and turned to Charles. 'Do you think we'll ever find out what happened to Tina's baby?' he asked.

The boy shrugged. 'If the calf is alive, my father will find her,' he said confidently. 'And don't worry, her mother won't leave without her. The whole troop will stay behind and wait.'

Mandy pictured the wardens and the elephants working together to rescue the lost calf. 'What will you look for?' she asked. 'What are the signs that there's an elephant in the area?'

'Many things,' Charles explained patiently. Like his sisters, he was shy and polite, with the same deep brown eyes and soft voice. 'We listen carefully. An elephant is a noisy eater. He shakes the trees and bushes as he pulls at the branches. And we look. There will be mud on a tree trunk, perhaps, where an elephant has rubbed against it. And his dung on the ground can tell us when he was there.'

She nodded eagerly. 'And how long before a young one like this begins to grow weak?'

Charles considered the question. 'Not many days. Evie is under two years old. I remember, because we looked after her here at the lodge when she was born.'

'Mandy!' James tried to remind her that it was time to go. The grown-ups were gathering in the yard, slinging their bags on to their shoulders and listening to directions from Abekuna.

'Hang on a sec! How come?' she asked Charles. 'Why did you have to look after her?'

'Tina was sick, so she couldn't feed her baby.

She brought Evie here when she was about three weeks old.'

'What was she like?'

'This big!' Charles raised his hand a metre from the ground. 'She weighed only a hundred kilos.'

'Only!' Mandy gasped. 'What did you feed her on?'

'We gave her cow's milk until her mother was better.' He smiled. 'Pretty soon she was getting into mischief, raiding the food stores and turning on the tap.'

'How?'

'With her trunk.' He laughed.

'James, Mandy!' Adam Hope called for them to set off.

Reluctantly, Mandy stood up. 'Did *you* feed her?' she asked enviously.

'Yes. It was my job,' he said proudly. 'Since she went missing this week, I've been out each morning before school, looking for her. This weekend we'll all try again.'

'Mandy!' Mr Hope called yet again.

Charles got up from the step. 'Why not stay?' he said shyly to both James and Mandy. 'Help us to find Evie!'

* * *

Adam and Emily Hope agreed that Mandy and James could stay on at the lodge, while they went back to camp with Dr Kambo. But first they left firm instructions with them to look after themselves and only do what Matthew told them.

'It's a great chance for you,' Mandy's mum reminded her. 'It's an adventure and a real help towards the conservation effort.'

'Which needs all the support it can get,' Adam Hope put in quietly.

'Yes, but it's really important to take advice and not go off and do your own thing,' Mrs Hope said.

'We know you two only too well!' Her dad grinned.

'Mad-keen on saving animals, eh?' Dr Kambo asked. He stood patiently waiting for the arrangements to be made.

'You've got it! If there's an animal in trouble, call James and Mandy. We've lost count of their rescue missions back home!'

'Good vet material.' He nodded his approval. 'From what I've seen, you've both got what it takes.'

Embarrassed but pleased, James and Mandy promised to take care. 'Thanks, Mum! Thanks, Dad!' Mandy could hardly wait to set out on the elephants' trail once more.

'Meanwhile, we'll take that drive into Arusha,' Emily Hope reminded them. We'll ring your mum and dad, James, and let them know what you're up to. And we'll ask Levina to keep in touch with the lodge by radio. If there's any news, you can call the camp.'

Mandy nodded and hugged them goodbye. Then they took to the shade of the giant baobab tree and watched the small party set off in Matthew's jeep to meet up with Joseph. When the vehicle had vanished in a cloud of dust, she turned to Charles with an eager smile. 'When do we start?' she asked.

'Who would have thought that something as big as an elephant could get lost?' James said.

They'd spent the whole of Saturday afternoon searching for Tina to see if she could lead them to her lost calf. There had been no sign of her on the hill where they'd last seen her, so now they were down by the lakeside, waiting for the whole troop to come down to drink.

'It's a huge area!' Mandy reminded him with a sigh. She flopped down against the trunk of a tall thorntree, took off her cap and pushed her blonde hair back from her hot forehead. They'd covered what felt like miles of pale gold grassland, climbed the steep slopes between volcanic rocks and boulders under the hot, hot sun. Now she turned to Charles, standing in the shade with them. 'Are we sure they'll come down to the lake?'

He nodded. 'An elephant must drink every day. They come at dusk.' He gazed out across the sparkling blue surface, standing alert as James too flopped down for a rest.

'Aren't you tired?' James gasped.

Charles nodded.

'Here.' Mandy stood up and offered him a drink from her water bottle. 'How worried are you now?' A whole afternoon without finding any sign of Tina or Evie seemed to have made Charles even quieter than usual.

He pulled down the corners of his mouth. 'James is right. A creature as big as an elephant can't just disappear.' Without taking his gaze off the lake, he drank and handed the bottle back.

She wondered how he could be so patient, then glanced across at his father and the other two wardens who sat nearby in the shade of another tree. The three men squatted on their haunches, arms wrapped round their knees, saying little. She realised where Charles had learned how to take things so calmly.

They waited for almost an hour, as the sun began to sink towards the mountain range on the far shore. The long lake began to glint with golden light, and the shadows of the trees crept long and deep along the water's edge.

Many animals came to drink. A herd of dark wildebeest waded ankle-deep and lapped noisily, surrounded by slim black and white ibis who dipped their curved bills and drank daintily. Then, when the sky had turned a milky yellow, three giraffes came down from the hills.

Mandy saw them and held her breath. They were some of the strangest, most beautiful animals she'd ever seen, with their long necks and small heads, with those knobbly horns and big ears. They came slowly in single file, ignoring their audience, loping across the pebbles and straddling their front legs wide to bring their heads down to the water.

Then, as the giraffes finished drinking and raised their heads at the sound of yet more animals approaching the water, Charles signalled to Mandy and James to stay still.

'Elephants!' he whispered.

In the shade of the tree, Mandy held her breath and tried not to move. 'Tina's troop?' she asked.

'Yes. The one in front is Aisha.'

The first elephant appeared two hundred metres from where they crouched. She waved her ears as she headed into the water, wading in with a huge splash and swirl.

'She's only got one tusk!' James pointed out.

'She broke the other in a fight,' Charles told him. 'It'll never grow back again. But she's still the old lady in charge of the whole troop.'

'How old is she?'

'Older than my father!' he grinned. 'But she still likes to play.'

They watched as Aisha plodded deeper, her pale grey skin turning almost black as she lifted her trunk and squirted water over her head and back.

'Magwa . . . Dika . . . Sobo!' Charles named each elephant who came out of the bush and made for the lake. 'And the big bull elephant is called Moses.'

Mandy turned to look anxiously up the slope for more members of the troop. Two calves trotted out of the trees, linked by trunk and tail. 'Who are they?' she whispered.

'Tyaa and Oljori.'

'I'll never remember all their names!' They'd reached the water, pushing and tumbling, sucking with their trunks and squirting with loud, playful squeals. Altogether Mandy could now count thirteen elephants.

'Unlucky number,' James muttered. No others

were going to turn up, however hard they hoped. It meant that Tina must still be recovering from her injury, hidden in the hills. And the mystery of Evie's whereabouts still remained.

'What now?' Mandy couldn't hide her disappointment.

'We try again tomorrow.' Charles too seemed to have decided that there was no point waiting any longer. He left the shade to go and speak to his father.

But the movement drew the attention of the big bull elephant. He saw the boy's shape glide out from under the thorntree, shot out his trunk in warning, and brought single-tusked Aisha rushing through the water to join him.

'Uh-oh!' Mandy remembered what it was like to be charged by elephants. She didn't want a repeat experience, so she looked round for a place to hide. 'What about up here?' She pointed to the lowest branches of the tree.

James shook his head. 'No, an elephant could uproot that with its trunk!' Nowhere was safe if the troop decided to charge again.

Meanwhile, the younger calves huddled behind the adults. Aisha and Moses watched and listened, as Charles stood his ground. He murmured something to his father, who nodded and let him go forward.

'He's going right up to them!' Mandy gasped. 'That takes some nerve!'

Charles walked steadily on, knowing full well that the elephants were still on edge. Would they let him get near? Would they know him? Would they trust any human being ever again after what had happened to Tina?

Moses let the boy come close. He rumbled another warning, but he didn't twist his face and bellow with anger. Instead, he watched cautiously. Aisha too swished her trunk and decided not to act.

From a distance, Mandy and James saw how tiny Charles was beside the massive creatures. She noticed Matthew standing by with Abekuna and Huanga, ready to run and help if the elephants turned against him. But what could they do, she wondered. One swipe of his powerful trunk, one scoop of those giant tusks, would kill Charles before the men could take a single step.

The boy tilted his head and reached out a hand. Moses snaked his trunk above his head.

'Listen, he's talking to him!' James whispered. They were too far away to hear what he said, but he went on, edging nearer until finally he reached up and rested his hand on the bull elephant's shoulder.

'Come on!' Matthew broke the silence. 'It's safe now.' The troop had recognised Charles and accepted him, so the three wardens walked into the open to join him, with Mandy and James following close behind.

'Just as well,' James murmured. 'I'm glad they don't think we're all like the poachers; out to get them!'

Mandy agreed. She walked up to Aisha with as much courage as she could gather, but still her heart began to beat fast as she drew near.

Charles turned and smiled. 'Say *jambo*, Aisha!' The old female swayed her trunk at Mandy.

'*Jambo*!' With a shaking hand, Mandy patted the wrinkled shoulder, standing well clear of her one remaining tusk; it was almost a metre long, she guessed, which was nothing in comparison with Moses'. The bull elephant eyed her warily, sweeping his three-metre lengths of ivory from side to side.

'Don't be afraid,' Charles told her. He looked

relaxed as he waded knee-deep into the lake and threaded his way between the younger elephants. 'They won't hurt you.'

'Not now they won't,' she agreed. 'What did you say to them to make them change their minds?'

'Easy.' Charles gave one of his rare grins. 'I told them we were their friends!'

Dusk fell quickly in the African bush, and once dark, the night would be thick and black. Though Aisha and her troop had drunk their fill and gone on their way, Mandy and the others waited by the lake until the last minute, still hoping to see Tina and her calf limp slowly down to drink.

'It won't be safe if we wait much longer,' Matthew said. He pointed out a pair of hyenas stalking towards them down the grassy slope, yellow eyes glinting, ears pricked. Huanga raised his long stick, ready for them.

'In any case, Tina won't show up now.' Charles knew that she wouldn't risk it, however thirsty she might be. 'It's too dangerous to bring a young one to the water alone in the evening.' He looked as downhearted as Mandy felt.

'Tomorrow,' his father promised. 'We can try again.'

So they turned back towards the lodge, weary after their long day in the open. Mandy sighed as she walked, impatient for the night to pass so they could begin the urgent search once more.

'Tomorrow,' she echoed, turning to glimpse the bright orange sunset over the mountains.

Six

'*Shifta*!' Huanga came running into the Mulakesi's house early next morning while Mandy and the others were eating breakfast.

Matthew sprang to his feet. The two men spoke rapidly in Swahili.

'Huanga says the poachers are back,' Charles told James and Mandy. 'His brother saw them as he came down from Gamunde this morning. A gang of six men.'

'The same ones who attacked Tina?' Mandy wished she could understand what the wardens were saying. Huanga waved his arms and pointed towards the mountains. He mimed the action of creeping through bushes, then standing and aiming a spear.

Charles nodded. 'He says they've come back to find the wounded mother. They know she was limping badly, so they must think they can find her again and finish her off.'

'But that's so cruel!' she protested. 'What can we do?'

'*You* do nothing!' Matthew broke off from talking to Huanga and turned to them, his face serious. 'The *shifta* are dangerous men, and I promised your mother and father that I would keep you safe.'

'But—!'

He raised both hands to stop her. 'No. If you want to know how bad these men are, ask Charles. I don't have time to explain. We've decided to take the jeep into the mountains to try and head them off, but you kids must stay here.'

James bit his lip and frowned. 'Does that mean we can't go out looking for Tina and Evie this morning?'

The warden nodded. 'I'm afraid so.'

They followed him through the house out on to the porch as he found his hat and car keys.

'When can we start the search again?' Mandy asked. She knew the order was sensible, and she would never break her word to her mum and dad, but her heart went out to the two elephants in danger.

Matthew paused on the steps. Huanga and Abekuna already sat in the jeep, silent and tense. 'We'll radio a message to tell you when it's safe,' he promised. 'Charles, you take care of things here.'

The boy nodded.

'Help your mother, and look after your sisters. With luck we'll track down this gang before midday and send them packing, eastwards, out of the crater. They have no licence to kill the elephants and this is national park land. When they find out we're on to them again, they'll give up and go away.'

We hope! Mandy prayed silently. She couldn't bring herself to watch the three wardens set off up the track towards the mountain village, so she went over to the room she'd shared with Josephine and sat quietly on the bed.

'Don't worry.' A soft voice interrupted her anxious thoughts. It was Josephine, standing at the door with Ruth. 'My father will find them.'

She nodded. 'But it's hard to sit and do nothing.'

The small girl let go of her sister's hand and came up to Mandy. She sat on the bed, gazing shyly at her, then she reached out to touch her wristwatch. Mandy held the watch to her ear and let her listen to its tick. Her round face beamed with delight.

'Watch!' Mandy pronounced the word carefully.

'Watch!' Ruth pursed her lips and copied the sound.

Then Mandy tapped her own chest. 'Mandy!'

'Man-di!'

'That's good!' She tapped again; 'My name is Mandy!'

Ruth concentrated hard. 'My name is Mandi!'

Josephine and Mandy laughed. Josephine spoke in Swahili, Ruth nodded and tried again.

'My name is Ruth!' she said, proudly.

She'd chosen Mandy as her special friend for the morning. As the warden's jeep headed out of sight, Ruth took her out into the yard. She pointed to the dog asleep on the porch: 'My name is Jon-jo!' She led her across to Huanga's house and introduced her to his little girls. 'My name is Nor-a. My name is Mary!' The children giggled and joined in the game. Soon a whole band of them was showing Mandy round the lodge.

They named Abekuna's son and his pet mongoose. They taught Mandy the Swahili words for 'How are you? – I am well!' Throughout the naming game, Ruth kept firm hold of Mandy's hand and led her from house to house and back out into the yard.

'Where are we going now?' Mandy let herself be pulled and pushed towards the giant tree at the gate. The children wanted to play a game of hide-and-seek, she realised. They made her cover her eyes and begin to count. Then, giggling and whispering they ran out of sight.

Once she'd reached fifty, she opened her eyes. She saw James and Charles watching her from the porch, smiled at them, then went to look for the little ones. She found Mary squashed behind a water barrel, then Nora squirmed out from between two baskets full of washed clothes. Where was Ruth? Mandy went looking along the track that led to the lake.

She peered under bushes and up trees. Was that a giggle she could hear from the thick undergrowth? There was a sound of leaves being rustled, the crack of a stick. Mandy followed the sounds.

No, it was making too much noise. This was something bigger than a young girl. Something very big. There was another loud crack. Mandy stepped back, ready to retreat. The bushes shook, the grass was crushed underfoot. The smell was familiar; Mandy breathed in and recognised what the heavy, sweet scent was.

'Tina!' she whispered the elephant's name.

She came limping out of the thick trees towards the lodge. Her trunk swayed, her ears flapped as she made her dogged way up to Mandy.

Mandy felt the elephant loom up. Tina's skin was dry and dusty, the wound on her hind leg beginning to heal. She rumbled as she came. There was a moment of panic; should Mandy turn tail and run away from this giant visitor? Should she stand her ground? The bushes snapped and broke under her weight, the ground shook with every step.

'There, good girl!' Mandy looked her in the eye and saw that she wasn't angry, but frightened. She spoke in a soothing voice.

'There, no one's going to hurt you!'

Tina reached out and touched Mandy's shoulder with the tip of her trunk.

It was a magical moment, as Mandy stroked her. 'See, I'm your friend!' She felt honoured, struck almost dumb by the elephant's magnificence.

She heard Ruth break out from her hiding-place nearby and run to fetch Charles. Still she kept on talking to Tina and soothing her. 'You've lost your baby, haven't you? Can't you find her? Do you want us to help?'

The elephant turned her head the way she had come, then she swung back to face Mandy.

'You do; you want us to help!' Mandy understood. 'We came looking for you both yesterday, but we couldn't find you! You're a good girl; you came to fetch us instead!' She stroked the thick trunk and praised her.

Charles, Josephine and James came running down the track towards them. They stopped short at the sight of Mandy talking to the elephant, then they advanced slowly. Tina shuffled sideways, giving a squeal when she put her weight on the injured leg. She waved her trunk more urgently, turning away, then coming back again.

'She wants us to follow her,' Mandy whispered.

Charles nodded. He went up and greeted his old friend. '*Jambo*, Tina.'

She twisted her trunk round his shoulder, purring and rumbling back at him.

'Where did she come from?' James asked. He was staring up at her huge head, standing well clear of her tusks.

'From that direction!' Mandy pointed to the hill where they'd searched the day before. 'James, I'm sure she wants us to follow her. I think she wants to lead us to Evie!'

He nodded. 'But Mr Mulakesi said we can't leave the lodge.'

'How can we explain that to her? She's come for help, and she won't understand, will she? She'll think we're letting her down!'

He stared at the ground. 'I know, but—'

They were stuck, torn in two directions. For a few moments, they didn't know what to do for the best.

'Let me try and get a radio message to Charles's dad!' James suggested. 'You keep Tina here. Talk to her, give her water; anything!'

'What will you tell him?' Mandy grabbed at the idea. She saw Charles nod too, as he stroked Tina and bent to examine the wound on her leg.

'I'll explain what's happened here. And I'll find out if they've found the poachers yet.'

'He'll know what to do,' Charles said quietly. 'Tell him we think Tina's calf is trapped somewhere on Thorntree Hill. Ask him if it's safe for us to follow Tina there.'

James nodded and ran off.

'How does the wound look?' Mandy asked Charles.

'It's clean.' He nodded his satisfaction. 'In a few days it will heal.'

They talked quietly to Tina, trying to calm her as the minutes ticked by.

Then James came running back with fresh news. 'I made contact!' Sweat trickled from his forehead, his T-shirt stuck to his back and he gasped for breath.

'Where are they now?' Mandy had gone a few steps to meet him. She held on to his arm.

'In Gamunde.'

'Did they catch the *shifta*?' Charles asked, sticking close to Tina's side.

'Not exactly. They saw them just below the village, making secretly for Thorntree Hill. But the minute the poachers spotted the warden's jeep, they turned and ran into the mountains. Mr Mulakesi says they lost sight of them.'

Mandy sighed. 'What happened next?'

'Huanga thought he recognised one of the boys in the gang. He lives in Gamunde. So Mr Mulakesi said they should drive to the village and speak to the boy's father, tell him what his son was up to.'

'Good.' Charles thought it was a plan that might work. 'The father will make his son obey the laws of the national park. It's a big disgrace for a family to be involved with the *shifta*,' he said, solemnly.

Mandy kept hold of James. 'Did you get a chance to tell them that Tina was here?'

He nodded and drew in a lungful of air. 'I asked if we could go with her up the hill and look for Evie. He said yes, as long as we keep out of danger!'

Mandy felt her whole body flood with relief. But they had no time to waste. Charles heard the news and began to turn Tina round in the narrow clearing, giving commands in Swahili, telling her to lead them where she wanted to take them.

'Your mother said you had to be careful, too!' James told him from behind, as they set off across the long, dry grass, following in Tina's giant footsteps. 'And Josephine and Ruth said good luck!' he told Mandy quietly.

They faced the sun and began to trek across country, away from the tracks, with the lake below them and a flat ridge of hills in front. A group of inquisitive baboons crossed the slope ahead of them, small ones riding on their mothers' backs, big males guarding the families from the strange sight of an injured elephant leading a girl and two boys into the wilderness.

'Poor Tina, she can only go slowly!' Mandy saw how painful it was for the mother elephant to make the journey. Often she would stumble and groan, then Charles would encourage her to keep going, through the thick thorntrees that gave the hill its name, leaving behind the wide stretch of open grassland where they'd searched the day before. Still Tina went on, higher up the hill, leading them forward.

Once or twice, Charles stopped to inspect a bush that had been crushed, or an unmistakeable pile of elephant dung. From it he could tell that this was the path Tina had used to find her way to the lodge earlier that morning. 'Still fresh,' he said quietly, watching her stumble on.

'That means she's deliberately leading us back the way she came,' Mandy said. Her legs ached, her face pricked in the heat of the sun, but she refused to rest. Instead, she struggled to catch up with the elephant.

'Yes. She's the only one on the hill today.'

'Where's the rest of the troop?' James turned to scan the hillside and the distant lake. They had risen far above water level, and the trees were growing sparser, the hillside more rocky.

'Down there.'

'Where?' He looked in vain. The shore of the lake seemed deserted, except for a pink band of flamingoes wading in the shallow water.

'By the baobab trees.'

James stared hard. 'I can't see them.'

'No, but they're there.' Fixing his own gaze on the ridge of rocks in the near distance, Charles strode on.

'Look at Tina!' Mandy said suddenly. She sensed a change as they drew near to the top of the ridge. The elephant was struggling more than ever up the steep slope, but she was pushing herself forward, dragging the back leg, crashing against boulders in her hurry. She seemed not to notice, but staggered on, her trunk thrust out, her head craning, as if she was listening to something that Mandy couldn't hear.

'Shh!' Charles warned Mandy not to race ahead.

'What is it?' James stared at the line of red rocks. Giant cacti stood like weird candlesticks along the skyline, and mounds of ant-hills reared up to left and right. 'What's happening?'

'The calf is somewhere nearby,' Charles told them. His voice stayed calm, but his body tensed as they all strained to look and listen.

Tina reached the top of the hill. The sun blazed down on her dusty grey back, her ears flapped as she called with a low roar for them to follow.

'Let's hope we're in time!' Mandy scrambled over boulders, between the ant-hills, feeling the rough volcanic rock beneath her feet. 'Come and look at this!' she cried.

At the top of the hill, the land fell away steeply into another valley. It rolled from under them, stretching down into empty, dry plains too barren for the zebra and impala to graze on. Mandy's heart had sunk at the sight of it; it seemed to stretch for ever, without trees or water. If Tina wanted to lead them down there, how would they ever be able to follow?

But she turned and trod the ridge, waving them after her with her trunk. A hundred metres, two hundred metres along the narrow summit of the hill, until they came to a clump of cactus and thorntrees; and beyond it, a deep split in the rock. Here Tina stopped dead.

Charles, James and Mandy came up alongside

her. They stared across the gulley. It was too wide to leap. There was no way across. Why had the elephant brought them to a dead end?

Tina thrashed the air with her trunk. She moaned softly and went on to her knees, sinking forward into the red dust. Mandy dropped down beside her. 'I think there's something down here!' she whispered. The shadow of the deep gulley sent a cold shiver down her back.

'What can you see?' James leaned over her shoulder. The split in the rock went down further than they *could* see; wide enough for someone to fall down; too deep for them ever to climb back out.

'Nothing. Wait – yes, there's something down here. It's pale, so it shows up in the dark!'

Now James and Charles were both on their hands and knees, trying to make out some white shapes in the black shadows. Tina moaned and cried.

'Oh no, that's terrible!' Mandy made out what the shapes were. 'Bones!' Huge, dreadful bones that could only have belonged to an elephant. They gleamed white in the darkness; a hollow-eyed skull with its long curved tusks, ribs and leg bones.

'Evie!' James's voice echoed along the gulley. They were too late. Tina's calf had fallen. She was dead.

'No.' Charles rested back from the edge, alert to every movement and sound. 'The bones are too big. They belong to an adult elephant. He's been there many months.'

Mandy grasped at the straw of fresh hope. 'Yes! And look, Tina's still trying to show us something!'

Beside herself with fear, the mother elephant had reared up and stumbled along the edge of the gulley, up against a pile of loose rocks. She almost slipped and lost her footing, squealed and fought to regain her balance. Below her, out of the deepest darkness of the split in the rock, came a weak, frightened scream.

'Evie!'

Seven

Mandy slithered on her stomach to the edge of the gulley. There was a drop of five or six metres, and the young elephant was wedged fast. As her eyes grew used to the gloom, Mandy could make her out, struggling to free herself, but too weak to move.

Charles tried to steady Tina. The mother elephant slid down the slope, away from the gulley, in a rush and grind of loose rocks. Eventually she came to a halt.

'How did she fall down there?' James crouched beside Mandy at the edge of the drop. Evie looked up at them, whining feebly.

'And when?' Mandy could hardly think straight. The calf waved her short trunk at them for help, but what could they do? She was out of reach, growing weaker. 'James, you don't think she's been down there ever since the poachers chased them?'

He nodded. 'Three days now. She must be terrified, poor thing!'

Mandy pictured the scene. 'They must have separated Tina from the rest of the troop and concentrated on her. That left Evie in a panic. She must have run up here looking for her mother, not seen the gap in the rock and crashed straight down.' There would have been a sudden drop into darkness, then Evie would have come to her senses surrounded by those awful bleached bones of the other poor elephant.

'Yes, and when Tina finally dragged herself away from the *shifta*, after Charles' dad had chased them off, she must have tracked Evie's movements and followed her up here.'

'I don't see how she did it.' Mandy could hear Tina struggling slowly back to the summit. She moaned softly, and Evie was whimpering a reply. 'We never heard anything, and we've been looking for more than twenty-four hours!'

'Maybe they do a kind of mind-reading,' James whispered. 'I've heard about elephants doing that. One thing we should be glad about, though, is that it looks like she didn't hurt herself in the fall.' He twisted round to ask Charles what he thought.

The boy rested his arm on Tina's trunk, trying in vain to calm her. 'Yes,' he agreed.

'So how do they do it? How *do* elephants stay in touch without making any sound?' Mandy insisted.

'They do make a sound,' Charles told them. 'But it's so low we can't hear it, that's all. What seems like magic is only them using their deep voices to talk to each other.'

'And that's how Tina found out where Evie had fallen?' Mandy was beginning to get over her first shock. She was still peering down the gulley, trying to work out how they could get the baby elephant out. 'Listen, maybe we can get a rope and lower ourselves down there!'

'Good idea.' James looked around for a firm rock to anchor a rope. The slope was scattered with large boulders, but their best bet would be to tie it around the trunk of a small thorntree about two metres from the edge of the gulley. 'I'll go back to the lodge for ropes!'

He was about to set off down the hill when Charles stopped him. 'Two of us should go. There are hyenas.' He pointed along the ridge. A slight movement behind a rock showed that he was right. 'If I come too, we can fetch bottles of cow's milk for the calf, and food for her to eat.'

'OK, but what about Mandy?'

She pushed herself up into a kneeling position, feeling her skin begin to creep. Alone on the hill with a band of hyenas? 'I'll be fine,' she told them, in spite of her doubts.

'Tina will be here,' Charles said. 'They won't attack while the mother is around.' He looked anxious as he explained what they would do. 'We'll be as quick as we can.'

'How long?'

'Two hours, maybe two and a half.' He looked up at the sun. 'It's past noon. You can wait in the shade.' Quickly he pointed to the tree which James wanted to use to anchor the ropes. 'Don't worry about the hyenas. But if something goes wrong and we don't get back after three hours, you must bring Tina down the hill to the lodge.

Don't stay up here until dusk; it's not safe.'

Mandy listened and nodded. 'Will she come with me? Won't she want to stay with Evie?'

'You must persuade her. She'll trust you; you're her friend.'

Mandy promised to do her best.

'You're sure you'll be OK?' James asked. 'I could stay here and let you go with Charles if you like.'

'No. I'll be fine, honestly.' She managed a smile. 'With Tina around to look after us, no hyena would stand a chance!'

So Charles and James headed off down Thorntree Hill and were soon out of sight. Mandy was left alone with Tina and Evie.

The sun blazed down and baked the rocks. The heat bounced off the ridge and drove Mandy under the tree for shelter. Tina, though, refused to leave the edge of the gulley. Soaking up the fierce sun's rays, she stayed to show Evie that she wouldn't desert her again.

Once or twice, as the afternoon wore on, and the whole landscape shimmered, Mandy ventured out to stand beside the mother elephant. She took her water bottle and poured a little water into her palm to let Tina drink.

She felt the soft tip of the elephant's trunk suck up the moisture, then the trunk would curve back and let the drops fall into her mouth.

'Don't worry,' Mandy whispered softly. 'We'll get Evie out sooner or later. Charles and James will be back with ropes and food. It won't be long now.'

Along the ridge she thought she heard a low growl. Could it be more hyenas gathering, waiting for nightfall? She stared down the hill, wishing that her friends would hurry up. An hour went by, then two. Evie continued to whimper from the deep gulley.

At last, two small figures reappeared at the edge of the lake and began to scramble up the hill. It was the two boys running as fast as they could, carrying lengths of rope and a rucksack that held the food and drink for Evie.

Mandy saw them from the ridge and felt herself sag with relief. The waiting had been horrible; watching Tina fret and hearing Evie whimper, sensing the savage hyenas keeping up their patient waiting game. Now help was coming. She stood up and went to stroke Tina's cheek. 'See, I told you,' she whispered. 'I knew

Charles and James wouldn't let us down!'

'You OK?' James gasped. He reached the ridge and flung the ropes to the ground. 'How's Evie?'

'We'd better get down there quick. She's getting weaker all the time.' She saw that they'd brought two long ropes. 'What did your mother and sisters say?' she asked Charles as between them they began to tie the end of one to the nearby tree.

'They're glad we've found the calf. Josephine found a bottle for feeding babies. She says Evie will suckle from it.' Charles produced the feeding-bottle from the rucksack. 'But my mother says the news from Gamunde isn't good. Huanga radioed from the village to tell her that the *shifta* haven't been found yet. No one knows where they are!'

For a second, Mandy paused. 'They could be heading this way again, then?'

'Who knows? Men from the village have promised to help my father. They know the mountains. Soon the *shifta* will be caught.'

'Let's hope it's soon enough,' James cut in. 'Look, I'm making a slip-knot in this end of the rope.' He formed a noose and laid it on the rock at the edge of the gulley. Tina watched anxiously as they prepared to take food and drink down to her calf.

'I'll go!' Mandy stepped quickly into the noose before the other two could object. She pulled the rope up round her waist and tightened the knot. 'I'm the lightest!'

'You're not afraid?' Charles asked.

'No. Hand me the bottle!' She didn't stop to think about the danger now.

'You go first.' James thought ahead. 'We'll use the second rope to send stuff down after you. That'll leave both hands free for you to climb.'

She agreed, then leaned back to let the rope take the weight of her body. The thorntree creaked and rustled, but stood firm. 'Right!' Edging towards the sheer drop into the dark, she began nervously to abseil out of the sunlight into the shadows.

'Careful!' James crouched above. His voice echoed, his figure was black against the daylight. Mandy felt small stones dislodge under her feet and pepper down into the gulley. Evie gave a squeal of dismay.

'It's OK, they missed her! I'm going down to one side of her.'

'I meant *you* be careful!' he hissed.

'How far now?' Charles' figure appeared alongside James.

'Not far. Another couple of metres. Can you get the stuff ready to send down after me?' Her heart was thumping so hard she thought they must be able to hear its echo from way above. But gradually, inch by inch, she found her way into the narrow crevice where Evie was wedged. 'I'm there!' she called, craning her head to look up at the dazzling light.

'We're sending down the whole bag!' James warned. 'It's tied to the rope!'

'Yep, I can see it!' A bundle began to drop towards her. She found her footing and groped along the crevice towards the young calf.

'Give her the milk first.' Charles took charge of what she should do. 'Put the bottle into her mouth if you can, so she can suck!'

The bag swung within reach. 'Got it!' Mandy seized and unzipped it, sensing in the pitch blackness that she was now very close to the elephant. There was a strong smell from the poor, trapped animal. Mandy could feel the heat from its body in this cold prison. Taking the bottle from the bag, she reached out her other hand and groped her way forward.

When the tip of Evie's trunk met her fingers, she almost pulled away in fright. Then she steeled herself and spoke. 'Don't be afraid,' she said softly. 'Here's milk for you to drink!' She tried to focus in the dark, watching out for the gleam of the elephant's eyes. With her hand she could feel the dry warmth of her trunk and cheek. Carefully she slid the bottle's rubber teat into the elephant's mouth.

'How are you doing?' James called.

His voice seemed a long way off. 'Good!' she sighed. 'She isn't hurt, only weak. And she's starting to drink!'

Evie must have felt the milk drip on to her tongue. She closed her mouth over the teat and began to suck noisily. Mandy felt the bottle tug and tilt. It was empty in seconds. 'She's finished it!' she called up to Charles.

'OK. Feel inside the bag. Can you find some bananas?'

She did as she was told. 'Yes. Shall I give her all of them?' There was a big bunch. Evie had smelled them and was poking her trunk into the bag.

'As many as she wants. There's sugar cane

and sweet potatoes too. Let her eat until she's full!'

'I don't think I could stop her even if I wanted to!' It took all of Mandy's strength to push the calf's trunk away from the bag. 'It's OK, she's eating the bananas,' she called. For a few moments, she stood back and listened to the sound of big jaws closing over the fruit.

'Good. Listen, Mandy, is there any way we can get these ropes underneath her?' James asked. 'If we could do that, maybe we could work out a way to lift her out of there!'

Mandy did her best to answer the question. 'I can't see much.' Evie's trunk snaked out once more. This time she fed her the long straight sticks of sugar cane. 'But I can try and feel if there's room.' She squeezed her hand along one of the elephant's firm flanks. 'No, I don't think so. She's struggled so hard to get out I think she must have wedged herself fast. There's no way we could get ropes right under her.' She sighed. 'Anyway, how could we lift her? She must weigh about five hundred kilos, remember!'

'Tina could pull her out,' James called down. 'But it's no good if we can't get the ropes in place.'

'No.' Her voice sounded hollow and flat. 'Sorry, James, there's just no way!'

'Has she finished eating?' Charles wanted to know.

She went back to the rucksack and fished out the lumpy shapes of sweet potatoes. 'Here's your pudding,' she said softly. Evie needed no second invitation. In a flash the nimble trunk snaked forward and the potatoes were gone. 'She has now!' she called back.

'OK, we're pulling you back up!' James gave up on his plan with the ropes. 'We'll have to decide what to do next when you get up here.'

'I think I should stay! Evie will be scared if I leave her!'

'Mandy, you've got to come up!' James insisted. 'It's going to be dark before too long. We can't just leave you!'

'But what'll we do?' For the first time since she'd been lowered into the gulley, she remembered the dry white bones of the dead elephant. She couldn't see them in the dark, but she knew they were there, further along the bottom of this death-trap. 'How are we going to get her out?'

'I don't know. We'll think of something.'

James' voice took on a worried tone. 'Come up, Mandy!'

She knew she had to do as he asked. But she stretched out one last time to stroke the calf's broad forehead. She could see the dark gleam of her eyes; not much more. 'You'll have to stay here a little bit longer,' she told her, 'until we can work out a way of lifting you out.' The baby elephant couldn't climb the steep sides of the gulley by herself.

Evie rumbled back at her. She snaked her trunk round Mandy's arm.

'No, I've got to go!'

Still the calf clung on.

'We won't go far. But we have to think, work out what to do next.' She talked as if Evie would understand, trying to stop her from being afraid.

But there was a catch in her voice as she managed to get free and tighten the rope round her waist once more. The gulley was a deep and dark place, frightening enough in itself. Then there was the problem of getting Evie out in one piece; and so far no one had come up with a plan that would work. On top of that, James was right about the light; it wouldn't be long before the sun began to set. Dusk meant danger. Hyenas were waiting out there, and who knew for sure where the sinister *shifta* were now?

'Don't worry,' Mandy said to Evie one last time. 'We won't let you down.' She steadied herself and planted her feet against the sheer side of the gulley. The rope took her weight. 'OK, I'm coming up!' she called.

Eight

James tried to keep their spirits up. 'Look,' he said, 'at least we've found out where Evie is, which we didn't know this morning. And you've given her some food and drink, Mandy. Now she won't starve to death.'

'But how are we going to get her out?' It must have been the fifth time that Mandy had asked the question. She sat under the thorntree, hands clenched around her hunched-up knees, staring at the edge of the gulley.

'We might not; not tonight anyway.' Charles stood gazing down towards the lake. The zebra had gathered to drink, and hundreds of gazelles, too. There was no sign so far of Tina and Evie's troop, though.

'I think we should try and persuade Tina to come down to the lodge with us for the night,' James suggested. He'd packed up the ropes inside the now empty rucksack.

Mandy sighed. 'That'll be hard. I can't see her leaving Evie alone all night, can you?' The mother elephant was still standing guard at the very edge of the drop. She looked like a statue, caught in the golden-red rays of the afternoon sun.

'Well, then, we'll have to leave her here.'

'And risk the poachers tracking her down again?' Mandy didn't know why, but she and James were on the verge of arguing. 'How can you even think that?'

He shrugged and slung the rucksack over his shoulder. 'I'm not leaving you here with them again, if that's what you think.'

Charles stopped watching the distant herds and came to talk to them. 'We've done well, but now we're tired. Let's go home.'

James nodded and jutted his chin.

'I can't!' Mandy whispered. 'I just can't do it!' She turned to the huge, still figure of the mother on the hill.

The others turned too. Leaving Tina wasn't something they wanted to do either. She was looking quietly at them, waiting for their next move. Then suddenly she flickered into life. She flapped her ears and tossed her trunk, shifting her great feet in the dust.

'What's wrong? Has she heard something?' James asked.

Charles signalled for them to wait and slipped away down the slope. Tina had begun to march up and down, like a sentry on guard. Mandy ran to her and stared hard down into the next valley. It seemed empty as before; dry and lifeless except for the flock of brilliant blue starlings that rose from the long grass and flew off.

'Maybe it's those hyenas?' James joined her. Tina was definitely upset about something. He looked for the heavy heads and spotted backs of the scavenging animals.

'Over there!' Mandy pointed to the rocks along the ridge. It seemed to be the hyenas' meeting place. 'I think I saw at least four.'

'You *think*!' James echoed.

'No, I did! I did see four!' She was sure it

hadn't been just shadows. Now, though, the rocks were deserted.

He shook his head and said nothing. 'Where's Charles got to?'

As he spoke, the boy's dark figure reappeared. He came up out of the empty valley, moving swiftly on to the ridge. 'Hyenas,' he reported. 'Six of them.'

Mandy bit her lip to hold back the taunt she felt like doling out to James. *See*! she wanted to say; *What did I tell you*? Instead she concentrated on the hunters who were slinking in for a kill. 'Is that what spooked Tina?'

Charles narrowed his eyes. 'No. Something else.'

'How do you know?' Once more she scanned the slopes to either side of the ridge.

'Because Tina's known about the hyenas ever since we arrived. She can deal with them, *hakuna matata*!'

James forgot his argument with Mandy and considered this. 'No problem? Hyenas didn't bother her, so what did?'

'Did you see anything else?' Mandy hated the idea that there might be more eyes out there, watching them. She began to imagine moving shapes in the long shadows, sounds of footsteps in the dry grass and scrubland below the ridge.

'No, they're too clever for that.' Charles strode up to join the worried elephant. Out of sight in the gulley, young Evie had begun to whimper and complain once more.

'They? Who's they?'

'I don't know yet.'

'Are you sure? Maybe we're all just getting jumpy because we're so tired,' James suggested. 'I know I am.' He pulled the hem of his T-shirt up to his face to wipe the sweat away.

'I'm sure. Tina hasn't seen anything because there isn't anything to see yet. But she's heard something and she's smelled something; look!'

They looked again, and sure enough the elephant's ears were still flapping and her trunk was raised.

Mandy agreed with Charles. 'Did you see the way those bright blue birds flew up?' she reminded them. 'What scared them, I wonder?'

'And see that!' Charles pointed to the hyenas' rocky lookout. Two of the creatures suddenly appeared at the summit and sniffed the air. Then they bounded out of sight.

Mandy caught her breath. 'If the hyenas are

frightened, what can it be?' She knew they would give way to lions, leopards or cheetahs, but nothing else.

'Down there!' Charles seemed to have decided that the danger came from further down Thorntree Hill. He pointed to more movements in the grass. 'James, you come with me. Mandy, stay here with Tina.'

Before she had time to object, he had taken James off down the slope. She watched them disappear amongst some bushes, and then let the silence set in. Her head was spinning, her thoughts were all over the place; hyenas prowling through the scrub, yellow eyes glowing. They came creeping out at her from every shadow. Or worse; a strong lion, a cheetah faster than the wind.

There's nothing there! she told herself, her teeth clenched. She stood in Tina's shadow, listening to the frightened murmur of the calf in the dark gulley.

There was a sharp crack. It came from behind a rock in the deserted valley, close to where the starlings had taken flight. Tina swung round to face it. Mandy stepped sideways out of her way, then waited. Nothing moved.

The waiting seemed to go on for ever. Then there was the soft rustle of something shifting in the sea of grass. Mandy's nerves had stretched to breaking point, when suddenly Tina went into action and launched herself down the slope, a great grey battleship ploughing through the waves.

A man stood up as the elephant charged. He was waist high in the grass; more of a boy than a man, dressed in a faded blue shirt and jeans. He shouted in Swahili, waving his arms at Tina to stop.

Shifta, poacher, killer!

Anger flashed through Mandy and she set off after the elephant, rushing into the grass, through sharp thorn bushes. Tina threw herself towards the boy, dragging her injured leg, trumpeting and lashing out her trunk at him.

There was terror in the boy's voice and face. His hands came up to shield his head.

In seconds Tina would have reached him and crushed him to the ground with trunk and foot. She would have gored him with her long tusks and tossed him to his death.

'No, Tina, stop!' Mandy raised her own voice above the thud and rumble of the elephant's charge. She ran to keep up, yelling as loud as she could. 'Wait!'

Tina heard her and obeyed. Within metres of the cowering boy she came to a halt.

'Good girl, Tina!' Trembling, Mandy kept on going. She drew level and reached up to steady herself against the elephant, who towered over the boy. He hid his face in his hands, and jabbered in his own language. 'It's OK, Tina won't hurt you now.'

Slowly he uncovered his face. He could almost feel the elephant's breath. He sank back on to his knees and stared up at her.

'Who are you?' Mandy demanded. If he was one of the poachers, he was very young; perhaps no more than fifteen or sixteen. He was small and slight, his hair was shaved close to his head and he wore a red bead earring in one ear.

'Eliud,' he gasped. 'My name is Eliud.'

His halting English reminded Mandy of little Ruth Mulakesi. And now she looked at him, she saw that he could be even younger than fifteen, perhaps still at school with boys like Charles. 'Listen to me!'

He dragged his gaze towards her from the

enormous wrinkled face and curved tusks of the angry elephant.

'Are you a poacher? *Shifta*? Do you belong to them?'

Slowly, realising he was cornered, he nodded.

'Eliud, do you live in Gamunde?'

Another nod. His chest heaved with fright, he shook all over.

'With your father?' This could be the boy who had been recognised by Huanga's brother. 'What are you doing with the poachers?'

He swallowed and shook his head, throwing her a sullen look.

'Is it your job to go ahead and scout for elephants?' she asked. He had no spear, she noticed, and he had been sent off by himself. There seemed to be no other *shifta* nearby.

Tina took one more step towards him.

He nodded and shielded his head once more.

Mandy put up a hand to restrain the elephant. 'What will you do now?' she asked.

'Make her stop!' he pleaded. He knew the dangers of the tusks, as well as their value to the *shifta*.

'Why?' she demanded. 'Why should I save you when I know you'll only go and tell your gang

where she is?' In any case, she didn't know if she could make Tina obey her for very much longer.

Eliud's voice choked in his throat. 'Please!'

She knew that not only the boy's, but Tina's life rested on her answer. If she let Eliud go, he would almost certainly give them away to the older poachers; the ones with spears and a greed for the dollars that Tina's ivory would bring. If she didn't, the elephant would take her revenge.

'Please!' he said again.

Mandy went forward and took his hands away from his face. She held them tight between her own. 'Eliud, if I let you go, promise me you'll go straight back to Gamunde!'

He stared at her.

'Go home to your father. Promise me!'

Behind them, Tina shifted again. Her trunk lashed the air above their heads.

'Go home and never join the poachers again! That's the promise you have to make!' She felt breathless and dizzy. Could she trust the boy? 'Promise!'

He pulled away from her, but she refused to let go. 'I promise!' he muttered.

'Straight home to your father!'

He nodded and twisted his arms free. Tina stood ready to curl her trunk round his slight body. Eliud froze again in terror.

'Go on, go home!' Mandy urged. 'And don't tell anybody where we are!'

At last he broke free of the terrified spell. He sank to one knee, then propped himself on his arms and stood up again. Tottering backwards, he cast Mandy a wild look.

What was that look? Was it gratitude for saving his life? Was it a look of scorn that she'd let him go? She couldn't be sure.

And now it was too late. The boy had broken away, had turned and was running down the hill into the deserted valley while Mandy kept a firm hand on Tina's shoulder. Then he was gone into the shrub, rustling through the grass, out of sight.

Mandy waited for what seemed like a long time. From the ridge, she heard James' voice calling for her. She turned and saw him with Charles. They must have come running from the other valley at the sound of Tina's angry bellow.

Would Eliud keep his word? She glanced again at the waving, shimmering grass, turned and walked up to tell the others what she'd done.

Nine

Mandy poured out her story. 'Did I do the right thing?' she asked Charles. 'What would you have done; let Tina charge him?'

Slowly he shook his head. 'I know Eliud Bawane.'

'He was just there in the grass. He's some sort of scout for the poachers. Why's he doing it?' She'd collapsed in the shade of the solitary thorntree on the ridge, gasping for breath.

'The Bawanes are very poor. There's no mother, the father is ill.' Charles stood alert at Tina's side.

'Will Eliud keep his promise?' James spoke

up for the first time. He too was exhausted. He took off his glasses to wipe his face.

Charles shrugged. 'Maybe. Or maybe he's too scared of the *shifta* and what they might do to him.'

'Such as?'

There was a long silence. 'These men kill elephants for money,' he reminded them. 'You don't need to ask what they'd do if they find out Eliud has betrayed them!'

Mandy took a deep breath. 'OK,' she said, 'what did you two see down there?' Whatever the boy did now, it was out of their hands. 'Was it just Eliud who spooked Tina?'

It was James' turn to break the silence. 'That's the really bad news,' he told her. 'There are more of them.'

'Where? How many?'

'All over the crater. Charles saw at least five men. I saw two. They were all on foot, and they had spears!'

'Did they see you?'

'No. So far as we could see, they don't know we're up here. They're still looking closer to the shore of the lake, waiting for Tina to go down to drink.'

'But they've come back?' Mandy's mouth had gone dry, her heart raced.

Charles and James both confirmed the worst. 'They won't give up,' Charles said. 'Not until they have their ivory!'

Mandy stared at Tina, standing guard over Evie once more. 'Neither will we!' she whispered. 'Whatever happens, neither will we!'

Shadows lengthened as banks of cloud settled on to the western hills and the sun sank behind them.

Now there was no question of the three of them persuading Tina to leave the gulley and come with them down to the lodge to spend the night there. They would never make it without attracting the poachers' attention for a start. No, their best bet was to stay where they were, hope that Eliud kept his promise and that the *shifta* stayed by the lake.

'Let's take it in turns to fetch food for Tina,' James suggested. He turned to Charles. 'What will she eat?'

'Most things.' He agreed with the plan. 'Fetch twigs and branches from the trees, but mind the thorns. They're very sharp. Fetch bark and grass, and any fruit you can find.'

'Two of us could go and one stay here.' Mandy was back on her feet, ready to set out. 'She'll need a lot of food, won't she?'

Charles volunteered to stand guard with Tina, as James and Mandy left the ridge.

'We'll be gone for ten minutes, no more,' she promised. 'If we take longer, we're in trouble, OK?'

'Watch out for *shifta*!'

She paused to stare down at the lake. 'Don't worry, we'll be quiet!' Then she ran with James to collect an armful of leaves and branches for Tina's supper.

They gathered the first lot of food from the bushes just below the ridge, pulling up shoots of the juiciest looking grass, tugging at branches to snap them off. Soon they had more than they could carry. They set off back to the top, creeping quietly across the bare rocks to where Tina and Charles waited patiently for them.

As the elephant seized a branch of thorn bush with her trunk and crammed it into her mouth, they set off again. This time it was Charles and Mandy's turn. They went lower down Thorntree Hill, keeping a careful watch. Mandy noticed how Charles moved. He crouched low, planting his feet firmly on open ground, skirting round areas of undergrowth where a hidden branch could trip him or a twig snap underfoot. She followed, tugging again at the leaves of an acacia tree, pulling up a fleshy root.

'How long before dark?' she asked. The shadows were creeping up the hillside as the sun sank lower.

'Half an hour.' Charles dug out more of the root with a knife which he took from his belt. Bending over it to scrape away the earth, he suddenly froze.

Mandy copied him. She crouched low behind a seisal bush and peered down the hill. The light was bad, her eyes played tricks on her; was that really a movement amongst the band of thorntrees below them? It could be an animal in hiding, scared by them as they foraged for Tina's food. It could be nothing. Or it could be *shifta*.

Charles' eyes glistened. He took shallow breaths, lowered the branches and shoots quietly to the ground. Silently he pointed to the trees.

Two dark figures wove in and out of the trunks. A spear caught the light and flashed from the shadows. Mandy gasped and bit her lip.

He pointed again. Wide of the trees, over to the right, three more men prowled across the hillside.

Eliud! He'd let them down, gone back and told the poachers that the injured elephant was on the ridge. Now they were closing in for the kill.

Charles signalled her to follow him. Though the men were on the right track, they hadn't yet seen exactly where Tina was. He beckoned Mandy urgently back to the ridge.

'They're coming up!' she whispered to James as she reached the top. Tina sensed the fear in her voice. She strained to hear the slightest noise in the valley. 'What are we going to do?'

'Hush, Tina!' Charles laid a hand on her. Down in the gulley, they could hear Evie trying to struggle out of her trap. Loose stones rattled, she gave a muffled squeal.

'What are we going to do?' James stared into the gathering dusk. 'We can't hide Tina, can we?'

Mandy came up with the only option left. 'We have to try and lead her down into the next valley!'

'She won't go!' James didn't believe she would leave Evie now.

'Let's try,' Charles said. He turned to talk to Tina in his own language, coaxing her away from Thorntree Hill.

But the elephant stood her ground. She planted her feet on the ridge, next to the gulley. Danger or no danger, she would stay where she was.

'Please, Tina!' Mandy joined in. 'We can come back tomorrow. You have to come with us. The poachers will find you, and this time we won't be able to stop them!'

She flicked her trunk and lowered her huge head. In the dusk light she looked black. Her tusks gleamed white.

Then the men broke from the cover of the trees. Three, four, five of them stepped out into the scrub and stared up the hill.

'They've seen us!' James cried.

Tina raised her head and trumpeted loud and clear.

Two other men appeared on the rocks where the hyenas had hovered. Three more approached from the deserted valley.

'We're surrounded!' Mandy's blood ran cold.

Shafts of red light from the dying sun touched the hill where they stood.

Silently the poachers moved forward. They could see their prey; the elephant they'd hunted for three long days. Children would not stand in their way, or stop them from killing her and stealing what they wanted.

Tina roared again. She screamed with anger as she recognised the men who had wounded her. But she too was torn; she couldn't leave the calf's side and take her revenge on the hunters. So she quivered and roared with rage at them as slowly, silently they made their way to the ridge.

Then, out of nowhere, there was a different roar. At first Mandy thought it was another elephant; perhaps Aisha or Moses coming out of the valley to help at last. Had the rest of the troop heard Tina's cries and come to chase off the poachers?

But no; the roar grew louder. It sounded like a machine; a car engine, as it whined and roared nearer and nearer. The *shifta* stopped dead in their tracks.

Mandy put her hands to her ears, deafened by the sounds. Tina bellowed in helpless rage, the jeep careered up out of the deserted valley, lurching over the rough ground at breakneck speed.

'It's the wardens!' James came to his senses first. He clutched on to Mandy and dragged her round to see.

The jeep churned up red dust as it screeched to a halt on the ridge. Huanga, Abekuna and Matthew jumped down and ran towards them. A fourth figure stayed inside the car.

'Oh!' Mandy fell on to both knees, battered by fear, anger and relief. She couldn't speak, as the men's feet crunched by. They stood guard around Tina, legs wide apart, hands on hips, waiting to see what the poachers would do now.

The shadowy men formed a group. They looked up at the wardens who stood in their way. From their distance of fifty metres they could have raised their spears and come on regardless. Mandy heard one man speak loud and fast. Was it an order to attack? Again she blocked her ears. She let her head sink forward, too frightened to look.

After what felt like hours but could only have been seconds, she felt a hand take her by the wrist and pull her to her feet. It was Charles, pointing down the slope. 'It's OK, they've gone,' he told her quietly.

The hill was empty as the sun finally sank behind the far ridge and plunged them into darkness.

Eliud Bawane waited until he was sure that the poachers had left for good before he stepped down from the jeep into the glare of Matthew Mulakesi's torch beam. He hung his head and scuffed the ground, waiting to see what they would say.

'How— What— ?' Mandy tried to make sense of the last half hour. 'Eliud, did you go and fetch Mr Mulakesi?'

The boy nodded. He stayed where he was, well out of Tina's range.

Charles's dad explained what had happened. 'We'd given up on the poachers after we lost them in the mountains. We asked around in the villages, but no one was telling us anything. Most people up there hate the poachers, but they prefer to mind their own business. As far as we knew, the *shifta* had given up the chase and headed off north.'

He examined Tina as he talked, anxious to

see that she hadn't come to any harm. 'Abekuna and I were busy picking up information about the elephant migration so that we could pass it on to Levina, while Huanga visited his brother. Anyway, young Eliud came staggering up the track nearly dead from running. When we could get out of him what was the matter, he told us everything we needed to know; where Tina was, where the poachers were, the danger you lot were in.' He inspected the wound above Tina's knee. 'This is healing nicely,' he said.

'You should have seen Matthew's driving!' Huanga laughed. 'We flew down the mountain and back up this hill!'

'Just in time,' Mr Mulakesi growled. 'And thanks to Eliud here.'

'Yes.' Mandy knew how hard it had been for him to do what he did. 'Thanks.'

He glanced up, then back at the ground. 'I made a promise.'

'Thanks anyway,' she insisted. 'Will you get into trouble?'

Eliud shrugged.

'Not while we're around,' Mr Mulakesi promised. 'We're bringing in the police to sort things out now that we've got names to give them. From now on there should be much less poaching in Ruwenzori.'

Mandy sighed. It looked like they owed Eliud even more than she'd realised. 'All we have to do now is get Evie out. Then we can let Mum and Dad know everything's OK.'

They gathered at the edge of the gulley, while Huanga turned the jeep to shine its headlights towards them. But Tina shifted uneasily in the strong beam.

'Kill the lights!' Charles told him, holding on to the elephant.

They had to peer into the dark split in the rock, listening for movement. Mandy described how she'd lowered herself down to see what was happening and to feed the calf.

'You say we can't get ropes under her?' The head warden crouched at the edge.

'No way. Anyway, she's wedged in one corner, and she's scared stiff.'

'Isn't this where Aisha's sister went missing a few years ago?' Abekuna recalled the incident. 'She disappeared somewhere up here. No one ever knew what happened to her. Not poachers, we knew that. It was a mystery.'

'Not any more,' James said quietly. He got

Matthew Mulakesi to shine his torch along the gulley to where the bones of the dead elephant lay.

The men studied it in silence.

'That's not going to happen this time,' Mandy said. 'We'll think of a way!'

'We may need more help.' The warden backed off from the edge. 'For now, we must go back to the lodge and get some sleep.'

'No!' Three voices spoke out; Charles, James and Mandy refused to leave.

'We can stay here now that the poachers have gone,' James said.

Mr Mulakesi listened to their reasons. He agreed that looking after Tina was their priority. He told them he had tents and sleeping bags in the jeep and he would leave the radio transmitter with them overnight. Soon they were unloading the equipment and pitching tent.

'Build a fire,' Huanga suggested. There was a bustle of activity as guy-ropes were tightened, wood gathered, food brought from the jeep.

Meanwhile, Abekuna radioed the lodge to explain the new plan.

At last everything was set up and the fire was

lit. Tina watched from a distance, a huge, shadowy figure on the ridge.

'Will she sleep?' Mandy asked Charles. They gathered round the fire as a wind got up and blew loose dust against their tents.

'Not much. She'll stand there all night. She won't leave.'

'Well, you need some sleep, even if Tina doesn't,' his father reminded them. 'Leave her to stand guard, rest as much as you can. Tomorrow morning, soon after dawn, we'll bring the jeep up to see what we can do.' He turned to Eliud, who had been keeping in the background as they built the camp. 'Ready to take a lift with us?' he asked.

Mandy stood up and left the bright circle of the fire. 'Would you rather stay?' she said quietly.

Eliud frowned. He looked puzzled.

'We'll need lots of help.'

James and Charles looked round, waiting for his answer.

'We'd like you to,' she insisted.

He shuffled and stuck his hands in his pockets, still not sure whether to believe her. 'You're not angry?' he mumbled.

'Not now.'

'OK!' Suddenly he grinned. The wind fanned the flames and lit up his face. 'I stay in a tent?'

'With me,' Charles said, standing up to join them.

'I never sleeped in a tent.'

'And James and I never saved an elephant!' Mandy laughed. 'This is a first for all of us!'

'Talking of sleep—' James yawned. The fire glowed on their faces, making them drowsy.

Charles had waved his father, Huanga and Abekuna off down the hill. Now he stirred the fire with a long stick and made sparks fly. 'I got your sleeping bag,' he told Eliud, pointing towards one of the tents.

'Sleeping bag?' He gave another frowning, puzzled look.

'A bag for sleeping in, with a big zip; look!' James went and fetched it for him.

Fascinated, Eliud tried the zip. He whizzed it up and down, then felt the padded softness of the bag. 'For sleeping in?' Clumsily he stuck his legs inside and grinned. 'In a tent, in a sleeping bag!' Gathering the bag round his waist and hopping over to where he was to sleep, he looked like a boy in a school sack-race.

Charles smiled. 'See you tomorrow,' he told

James and Mandy, then followed Eliud to the tent.

'Another big day.' It was James' turn to look longingly towards his own tent. 'Time to turn in, then?'

'I'm OK here for a bit,' Mandy told him softly. She stared into the embers. 'You go and get some sleep.'

'Your mum and dad will be pleased.' He got up and stretched. 'Don't stay up too long. I'll see you in the morning.'

Mandy nodded and watched him go. She was tired, but she waited until the fire had died down. There was no movement from the other two tents, and Tina stood quite still. In the gulley Evie made no sound.

How would they get her out? If ropes wouldn't do, what else was there? She racked her brains to come up with an idea. As she stood up to go to her tent at last, she noticed the light cast by the bright moon on the slope where she stood. Thorntree Hill looked strange; drained of colour, rocky and uneven, covered in loose boulders, like the surface of the moon itself.

Rocky! Loose boulders! Idly she lifted her foot and kicked one. It shifted and she bent to see if she could lift it. *Heavy, but not impossible*, she thought. She kicked another and another. It was late; there was no one to talk to, but she felt an idea begin to form.

Slowly she went to her tent and crawled inside. *I think we can do it*! she told herself. *Please, please let it work!'*

Ten

In the grey light of early morning, as the dawn mists rolled down the sides of the crater, the four of them began the final rescue attempt.

'Let's not wait any longer!' Mandy had pleaded after she'd explained her idea. 'We can start, then when Charles's father and the other wardens come back, they can join in.' She knew it would take many hours for the plan to work.

Tina still stood watch. Her night had been long and lonely, but as dawn broke she could see the dim shape of her calf in the bottom of the gulley and hear her soft moans as she pleaded for help. Now she looked on as Mandy and James began to drag and roll boulders on to the ridge.

Charles hesitated. 'I'm not sure,' he protested. 'Tina won't like what we're doing.'

'She will when she understands.' Mandy dragged a large rock to the edge of the drop, then stood up to ease her aching back. 'Once she sees the point of it, we might even get her to help!'

Eliud agreed with Charles. 'No elephant is clever enough.'

'Tina is,' she insisted. 'Look, the plan is to tip the rocks down this end of the gulley, well away from Evie. We have to make a sort of ramp for her to climb up by herself, bit by bit!'

'It's going to take an awful lot of rocks,' James pointed out. He looked at his hands. They were already scraped and bruised by the work he'd done on the first few. 'There's a five-metre drop to fill up!'

Mandy had to convince them that it was worth going on. 'OK, I know it'll upset Tina until she understands what's going on. But I've thought of a way around that.' Quickly, she fetched the rope which she'd kept from the day before. She went to sling it around the tree trunk and tie it in a firm knot. 'I'm going down again to look after Evie,' she explained. 'If I'm in there with her, Tina will know we're trying to get her out!'

'That's dangerous!' James stood in her way. 'Honestly, Mandy, who knows which way the rocks will fall?'

'If we're going to risk it for Evie, we'll have to risk it for me as well.' She looked him in the eye, silently challenging him to come up with a better idea. 'Anyway, we know she's stuck fast down there, so unless I can help her get free, she's there for good!'

Charles listened to them and thought it through. 'I think Mandy should go down,' he said quietly. 'We'll carry on bringing rocks up here while she sees what she can do to help the calf. Take food down with you,' he suggested. 'Evie will do anything for green shoots or leaves.'

Mandy nodded. 'OK?' She wanted James to agree. It was a life or death situation for the young elephant, but she wouldn't do it until James and she were on the same side. 'We've got to try!' she pleaded.

At last he took a deep breath and nodded.

'Great!' She stepped into the circle of rope

and slipped the knot tight round her waist while Eliud went to gather fresh tips from the thorn bushes. He tied them into a bundle and waited to lower them down to her.

When she was ready to begin, poised on the edge of the gulley with the rope taking the strain, Mandy paused. 'Here we go!' she said to Tina, who stood close by. The elephant's gaze was steadily on her. 'This time we're really going to do it!'

Then she eased herself into the gulley for the second time, feeling the cold shadows swallow her, hearing the whimpers of the trapped calf, seeing Tina hovering at the brink. Mandy let the rope take her weight as she found footholds. Once she slipped and sent a shower of pebbles sprinkling down. She recovered and went on until at last her feet touched the bottom.

'OK, I've done it.' She called up to Eliud for the bundle of food and caught it as the rope snaked towards her. 'I'll need a torch to see what I'm doing!'

'There's one in our tent.' Charles ran and fetched it while Eliud pulled the rope back to the surface. They tied the torch on the end and once more lowered it to Mandy.

'Thanks!' She caught it neatly. 'Give me a few minutes to get Evie free, then we can start building the ramp!'

The torch flicked into life as she pushed the button. She shone the beam down at her own feet to see that the bottom of the gulley was heaped with loose stones and dry branches. Further along, as the space grew wider, she saw bigger rocks mixed with broken bones; sad reminders of the earlier accident. Behind her, as the gulley narrowed and ended, poor Evie was wedged in the corner, her trunk flailing as the torch caught her in its yellow beam.

'It's OK,' Mandy whispered. She edged towards the calf with one of the tasty branches. 'Remember me? I've brought you some more food.'

Evie sniffed and reached out with her quivering trunk. Mandy held the branch just out of reach. 'Come on, come and get it!'

The calf stretched, tempted but unable to shift. She cried to be fed.

So Mandy gave in and let her have a first taste. She watched Evie grab the branch and shove it into her mouth, chewing noisily. When she'd finished, they began all over again.

'Come on!' Mandy made her reach a little bit further the second time, then further and further still. Every time she made the calf crane forward, she heard her sides scrape against the rock to either side, saw her weight shift a fraction. At the fifth attempt, she stretched and slid forward a couple of centimetres. Now her front end was free and only her back end was wedged in the corner. 'That's it! One more time.' Mandy prayed that this time they would make it.

And sure enough, as she shone the torch on Evie's stumpy back legs and made her stretch for the food, she saw her ease herself free. The calf tottered and fell on to her knees, then raised herself up to snatch the branch.

'We did it!' Mandy yelled to anyone who was up there to hear. 'James, she's free; we did it!'

A head appeared at the rim of the gulley. 'Brilliant! Is she OK?'

'It looks like it. She's wobbly, but she's stuffing herself with food again!' Flashing the torch up towards the daylight, Mandy caught James' face in its beam. 'That was the easy bit,' she reminded him. 'How are you doing with those rocks?'

'We've got a good pile already. Tina's started to help. She's shoving the biggest ones with her trunk. When do you want us to start tipping them down?'

'As soon as you can. Let's see if it's going to work.'

'Listen, you've got to stand well back, OK?' His voice sounded hollow as he peered anxiously down.

'I'll shine the light to let you know exactly where we are. Send the smaller rocks down first, until Evie gets used to the noise!'

James organised it from above. His head

vanished for a while, then reappeared. 'We're ready!'

'OK then, so are we!' She held her breath, bracing her arms against the sides of the narrow gulley so that Evie couldn't pass, praying that the calf wouldn't rush forward and trample her in her panic.

'Here comes rock number one!' he warned.

Mandy looked up. James, Charles and Eliud shoved the rock to the very edge. She heard a grinding noise, saw it wobble, tilt, then drop. It fell with a shower of dust and pebbles, bounced against the gulley sides, then thudded to the ground about ten metres from where she stood, wedged tight between the sides.

'Hold it!' She struggled to hold Evie back. The calf had squealed at the falling rock and was shoving with all her weight. 'Hush! It's OK, see. Everything's fine!' She soothed her then shouted up to the others. 'How's Tina?'

'Not happy,' James said. 'She's making weird sounds.'

'She's talking to Evie,' Charles told her. 'Show them what we're planning to do!'

So Mandy shone the torch on the fallen rock and clambered towards it, past the crushed bones, dry branches and piles of pebbles. She set one foot on it and stepped up. The rock raised her by fifty centimetres. 'See!' She showed the calf what she'd done.

Evie quietened. She seemed to be listening to her mother's voice, watching Mandy, trying to understand.

'Right, now I'm going back to the far end of the gulley,' Mandy yelled. 'Wait until we're ready!' She scrambled back to safety. 'OK!'

A second rock tumbled and landed beside the first. The noise filled their ears and frightened Evie again, but this time she struggled less. The boys pushed again; an even bigger rock came plummeting into the gulley. Then they paused.

'How's it looking?' James's head appeared up above.

Mandy shone the torch on the slowly growing pile. Through the rising dust they could all see that the ramp was beginning to take shape. 'Watch this,' she told them. Eagerly she scrambled to it and stepped up again. This time she stood a metre higher than before.

'Tina saw that!' Charles yelled down. 'I think she understands what's happening!'

Mandy could hear the mother elephant rumbling up above. Evie listened and waited.

'OK, now we can really get going!' James promised. 'Stand back, Mandy, and let's see how high we can make this thing!'

She did as she was told. Once she was safe with Evie at the far end of the gulley, the rocks began to tumble down in quick succession. Through the scraping, grinding rumble, she heard eager voices as the three boys encouraged Tina to help them shove more rocks to the top of the hill. Slowly the platform took shape.

'We're taking a rest,' James reported after half an hour's hard work. 'How's Evie doing?'

'She's fine. I'm going to show her how to climb up!' She warned them not to tip any more boulders over the edge for now. Then she led the young elephant forward, helping her to squeeze through the narrowest spaces, waiting until she found her footing and crept forward. It took patience to convince her that she was safe.

Then Mandy showed her how well they were getting on, finding footholds on the pile of boulders for her broad, flat feet, urging her to the top. After three days underground, as she raised her trunk towards the surface, Evie at last felt a breath of fresh air.

'Mandy!' Watching from above, James had more news. 'Charles's dad is coming up the hill!'

'Great!' Now they would have extra help. 'Eliud, can you send down some more food for Evie, please! I've got to get her down off here again!'

Their new friend went to collect leaves and grass, while Charles and James ran to meet the warden's jeep. Now only Tina's huge head hovered at the edge of the gulley, peering down at them.

'It's going to be fine!' Mandy told her. 'Just wait a little while longer and we'll have your baby out of here!'

And me too, she thought. Down in the gulley the dust had got up her nose and into her mouth. She felt grit between her teeth and in her throat. Her eyes watered as she blinked hard to clear them.

The wardens arrived in the jeep and willingly joined in with the plan. They got to work; three extra pairs of strong hands to lift, shove and haul the boulders into position before they toppled them into the crevasse. From the far end of the gulley, in the rapidly dimming light of Mandy's torch, Evie chewed at her fresh leaves and waited.

'OK, try it now!' James called down as the workers took a break. 'See how many more rocks we need.'

The pile was over two metres high, and now Mandy had to test it to see if it was steady. She went and climbed cautiously, testing where to put her feet.

'Watch it!' James heard the pile shift. A loose rock halfway up wobbled and fell.

Mandy lost her balance and felt the rocks give way. She flung out both arms and grabbed for a firm hold, scraping her knuckles and clutching at the solid walls. Eventually the small landslide came to a halt. 'I'm OK!' she called up. But getting Evie to climb the unsteady heap wouldn't be so easy. 'See if you can find as many flat rocks as you can, so they don't rock too much when we stand on them.' At this rate, the battery in the dimming torch would have died by the time they got out. She retreated to the far corner and tried her best to be patient.

It was hard work, even with the men's help. Now they had to look further afield to find suitable rocks and it took them longer to heave them to the edge. There were more gaps, the escape route grew all too slowly.

'Do you want us to pull you up for a bit?' James was worried about Mandy as the morning wore on.

She looked up at the sky. It was blue now, and fresh. For a moment she was tempted to leave Evie alone.

'I could come down instead.'

'No thanks, James. I'll hang on.' She wanted to stick it out and show the calf the best way up. So she stayed in the dark and dusty gulley while the work went on.

Towards midday Charles's face appeared. 'Try it now,' he suggested. 'I think it might be nearly high enough.'

A row of other faces lined up to watch as she tested the ramp. 'There are still a few loose stones,' she reported. 'But the whole thing feels safe!' As she climbed nearer to the light, she heard Evie follow her. She turned to see her planting her feet on the lowest rocks. 'Not yet,' she warned.

But the calf knew her way out and she decided she'd waited long enough. She refused to back down, waving her trunk at Mandy and urging her forward with impatient squeals and squeaks.

'It looks like you'd better let her try this time!' Charles gave the go-ahead.

'I don't think I can stop her!' She felt a shove from Evie's trunk. 'OK, here we go!'

Step by step they climbed up the ramp until Mandy reached the top. The pile of rocks stopped just short of ground level, but it was high enough for her to haul herself out. She felt the sunshine hit her face like the blast of heat from an oven; the light dazzled her as she pulled herself free of the crevasse and slumped forward.

Evie followed clumsily. Her weight sent loose boulders sliding, but she kept on coming, scenting the fresh air and hearing her mother's calls.

The rescuers waited, afraid that she would slip. Another fall could break her leg.

The tip of her trunk appeared, then the tops of her ears. More rocks crunched and slid. She took another unsteady step up on to the top of the ramp. Her eyes blinked in the strong sun as the rest of her head showed above the ground.

'Come on, you can do it!' Mandy urged. She lay down to help her climb the last little bit.

Evie wobbled and almost slipped.

Matthew and Huanga ran to fetch ropes, while Tina came forward and twined her trunk round the baby elephant's neck. She held her fast.

'That's it, Tina, now pull!' James saw that she could help the calf up the last big step.

She rested back and raised Evie on to her hind legs, pulled her forward so that her forelegs rested on the edge of the gulley. The wardens came with the ropes and began to tie them round Evie's legs, but Charles told them to wait.

Tina was still holding on, easing her calf out of the gap. At last, straining with every ounce of her strength, she lifted Evie clean off her hind feet. The calf's feet paddled, she squeaked with surprise as her mother drew her through the air and landed her safely on solid ground at last.

Eleven

'Fetch some water from the jeep!' Matthew
Mulakesi gave the orders amidst cries of joy and
congratulations. 'Stand back, give them space!
Just let's see what we're doing!'

Mandy grinned and did as she was told. James
had whipped off his baseball cap and thrown it
in the air. Charles and Eliud slapped the palms
of each other's hands like American football
players. Meanwhile, Tina fussed over Evie,
twirling her round with her trunk, inspecting
her for cuts and bruises. The calf was shaky and
confused but otherwise unharmed.

Huanga and Abekuna ran back to the ridge

carrying three plastic cans and an empty bucket. They sloshed water into the bucket and slid it towards the elephants.

Tina shoved Evie bossily forward to make her drink. Mandy heard the sucking noise as the calf dipped her trunk, curled it back and squirted a jet of clean, cool water into her mouth.

Again! Tina ordered her with another firm push. The little calf sucked and squirted. The water missed her mouth and dribbled on to the dry, hot rock.

Then it was the mother's turn. With her long trunk she sucked the bucket empty and shot the water expertly into her own mouth. James rushed to fill the bucket, just in time for Tina's trunk to snake back in and suck once more. This time she aimed at Evie's big head. The young one gave a squeal as the cold water splashed all over her.

Mandy and James stood back and laughed as Evie stood and dripped. She twisted her trunk and tried to suck up droplets from her ears. They were so busy watching her antics that they didn't see Tina's trunk dip into the bucket and take fresh aim. Suddenly they too were drenched.

'Aagh!' Mandy gave a scream. Her T-shirt and shorts were soaked.

'Tina, no!' Too late. James stared down at his squelching shoes. 'Why did she do that?' he gasped.

It was Charles and Eliud's turn to laugh. 'She thinks you're too hot; she wants to look after you.' Charles ducked as Tina got ready with another trunkful of water. Behind him, Eliud was the one who took the next full blast.

'I don't care!' Mandy took her cap off and squeezed it dry. 'Tina can splash me any time she likes!' Spray was going everywhere, rainbow droplets shining in the sun, as the elephant cooled everyone down.

'It's her way of saying thank you,' Matthew grinned. His expert eye checked the two elephants. 'They're certainly pleased to be back together.'

When Tina ran out of water, she stood quietly to let Evie feed. The calf snuggled behind her forelegs and suckled noisily.

'Just a few more weeks of that,' the warden told them, 'then the youngster will have to fend for herself.' He gave a satisfied sigh.

It was a perfect picture; the young elephant

and her mother reunited after their terrible ordeal.

'Now all we have to do is get them back with the herd.' The job wasn't quite over, Charles reminded them. 'We can't leave an injured mother and her baby alone up here.'

'No need to worry; look!' James pointed down Thorntree Hill towards another wonderful sight. A procession of elephants was plodding towards them, nose to tail, swaying from side to side. 'It's like magic!' he whispered.

'Mind-readers!' Mandy stood, hands on hips. 'How did the troop know the exact time when they could come and collect Tina and Evie?'

'They just knew.' Charles wasn't the least bit surprised. He went down to meet Aisha, the old mother of the troop, and guided them up the slope.

Soon Mandy and James were surrounded by elephants. Mandy reached out and touched Aisha's old, saggy skin and broken tusk. She thought she could read an expression in her eyes that said, 'Nothing in this world surprises me; not the wickedness of the *shifta*, nor the courage of Tina. I've seen it all before.' Then Aisha turned to marshal the herd.

James went to stroke Tina one last time. There was a throng of people and elephants gathered on the ridge, but Tina waited for him and wound her trunk round his arm. Her hide was warm and rough as he patted her and said goodbye.

Dika, Tyaa and Magwa shunted and pushed into position. Moses stood slightly apart. Eventually Tina managed to separate Evie from the other calves and tuck her alongside. The troop was ready to move off.

'Good luck!' Mandy whispered.

Tina acknowledged her with a turn of her head, a kindly look. Then Aisha gave the call and they went. One by one they left the ridge and returned to the valley, heading for shade and food, to wait until evening when they would go down to the shores of Lake Kasanka to bathe and drink.

That evening there was a great celebration at Ruwenzori Lodge.

Adam and Emily Hope had driven up with Levina after Joan Mulakesi had radioed the camp. Eliud's father came down from Gamunde to forgive the boy and take him back home, but Huanga made him welcome and offered them a place to sleep if they would stay and join the party.

At dusk, Abekuna brought out the drums, and music began in the cool yard in front of the lodge. Joan and Josephine brought food and drink on to the porch, while little Ruth did her best to keep Jonjo away from the dishes.

'Shoo!' She shouted and clapped her hands at the dog. Then she ran to Mandy to ask for help and drag her back to the porch.

Emily Hope was there, helping herself to rice and vegetables. 'Did you hear the latest news about the poachers?' she asked.

'No, what?' For a moment Mandy felt her skin prickle, until her mother laid a kind hand on her arm.

'The whole gang has travelled far to the west,' she explained. 'They've been seen retreating across the plain. I don't think they'll cause any more trouble to our elephants this year at least.'

Mandy took a deep breath. Tina and Evie were safe.

As the drums grew louder and Josephine led the girls of the lodge in a rhythmic dance, she went to pass the good news on to Charles, James and Eliud. The boys nodded with relief and went on chatting. They invited Mandy to join their action-replay of the rescue.

But she shook her head and drifted out towards the tall banana trees and stood in their quiet shade. She loved the music and the dancing, the laughing children and the smiling faces of the adults, but she wanted a few moments alone.

She gazed out at Thorntree Hill, watching the last rays of red sunlight disappear from the ridge. She felt small in this vast country; new and inexperienced in the ways of its people and animals. It had stood unchanged for thousands of years, and would be the same long after she was gone.

In the pale grass not five metres from where she stood, the round, dark eyes of a young gazelle stared at her. Mandy gazed back. She felt perfectly content.